Organized Chaos

Chaos Duet Book One

Drethi Anis

D1524399

Organized Chaos © copyright 2021 by Drethi Anis.
Copyright notice: All rights reserved under the International and Pan-American Copyright Conventions. No part of this book may be reproduced or transmitted in any form or by any means, electronic or mechanical, including photocopying, recording, or by any information storage and retrieval system, without permission in writing from the publisher.
This is a work of fiction. Names, places, characters and incidents are either the product of the author's imagination or are used fictitiously, and any resemblance to any actual persons, living or dead, organizations, events, or locales is entirely coincidental.
Warning: the unauthorized reproduction or distribution of this copyrighted work is illegal. Criminal copyright infringement, including infringement without monetary gain, is investigated by the FBI and is punishable by up to 5 years in prison and a fine of $250,000.

Author Note

For optimal enjoyment, dive into this book blind. However, if you are sensitive to dark subject matters, then please heed the warnings.

This novel contains dubious sexual scenes and discussions of mental health issues. It's an age-gap romance with an underaged teenager. Depending on your comfort zone, the content might disturb you.

If you plan to read The Quarantine Series, this is a friendly warning that you will stumble upon spoilers from the series.

Organized Chaos is the first of a duet and NOT a standalone.
ORGANIZED CHAOS
DISCORD

For my husband and dog. Thank you for being so patient while I ignored you to write this book.

I also want to acknowledge my wonderful team: Bibi, Ash, Allie, Angie & Leah.
And a special thank you to Kathy, Crystal, Maria, Kelly, Karen & Alexis for all of your support.

She waited all her life for the right guy.
Too bad she met the wrong guy first.

Brandon Cooper meets a mysterious woman, Maya Mathews, during a critical point in his life. What ensues next is a whirlwind romance between the two lost souls.

However, Maya's reservations spark Brandon's suspicions, indicating that a web of lies stands between them. As the situation intensifies, Brandon races against an invisible ticking clock in a desperate attempt to dig deeper into her life.

Brandon's only clue is Maya's connection to a little girl from his past.

Part one

Chapter 1

Karens ignore trigger warnings, only to later complain about said warnings. Don't be a Karen. This book contains dubious sexual scenes and mental health issues. It's an age-gap romance with an underaged teenager. Depending on your comfort zone, the content might disturb you. This trope is ONLY intended for open-minded readers interested in exploring their fantasies in the realm of fiction while exercising the good judgment to differentiate it from real-life situations.

Brandon

"Hello there," said the semi-corporate asshole.

He looked like one of those fresh out of college investment banker dicks. We all knew his type. Cocky. Self-assured. A 'Suit.' Chasing meaningless skirts. He was staring at the girl in front of him, presuming to have found his calling for the night.

The girl made quite the impression with her entrance, the way she glided inside the hotel bar. The place was filled with men traveling due to a convention, and the savages eyed her hungrily.

At the time, both Farah and Tasha were hitting on me, though they were barking up the wrong tree. Neither would be on my radar even if I were in a social mood, and I was far from jovial. My only date for the night—a bottle of Jack.

However, the effect of lonely souls must have been contagious because, despite my best efforts, I was inexplicably drawn to her as well.

She was an all-American beauty. Small frame with curves, legs elongated for miles by her heels. The golden skin suited her, complimenting locks of blonde hair. My mouth went dry every time she flipped the long strands over her shoulders.

Yes, the girl was easy on the eyes. However, beautiful women paraded the city of Nice. Factually speaking, she wasn't even all that remarkably pretty. I didn't understand the fuss, but the night suddenly seemed young and full of possibilities.

She was on the other side of the circular lobby bar as I dodged Farah and Tasha for a better look. The geometric shape of the structure allowed me to watch as the events unfolded.

"May I buy you a drink?" the cocky, self-assured asshole asked smoothly. I didn't care for the familiarity he sported—or the greedy eyes lapping at her figure—but clenched my teeth to stop myself from reacting prematurely. Irrational anger would only paint me as a psychopath.

Once the bartender sat down my whiskey, I grabbed the tumbler and scooted closer, taking a large gulp during my migration. Piercing blues locked intently with mine as she looked over to glance at me.

She is attracted to me.

The girl's smile didn't reach her eyes as she acknowledged the man's request. "I'm alright. Thank you."

That was the signal to take a hint. The song and dance set by the rules of society were straightforward. If a man offered to buy a drink and the girl rejected said drink, he had to politely move on to the next unsuspecting prey.

Not this man. "Oh, come on. Just one drink."

My fingers inadvertently twitched, lava churning inside my stomach. The fucker was blatantly hitting on her, and there was not a thing I could do to stop it. The impulse to remove her out of his sight was so immensely heart-pounding that I considered throat punching myself, hoping the pain would distract me from the ridiculous whim.

I reprimanded myself. Hitting on random women—or hitting people on their behalf—wasn't my style.

She let the man down gently once more, eyes drifting back to mine. "I really appreciate it, but I'm waiting for someone."

The man's face fell, and mine went into overdrive.

Did she just like the attention?

She had eye-fucked me while this douchebag hit on her. All the while, she was waiting for someone else entirely?

I hated women with such complexes.

"What idiot keeps a woman like you waiting?"

For the oddest of reasons, one I couldn't explain with a gun to my head, I burst out, "Guess that'd be me." I towered over the creep in two long strides, setting my glass down on the bar counter.

"Umm... hey, man," he fumbled awkwardly. "I didn't realize she was here with someone." He gathered himself and swiftly disappeared without a backward glance.

And that's why sheep shouldn't target a lioness.

Tilting my head, I eyed the lioness in question. I only arrived in France twelve hours ago. The last thing I expected was this... distraction. Though one sheep was out of the picture, there was another in the mix—the fucker she was waiting to meet.

However, she blew me away by snatching the question right out of my lips. "Finally! I've been waiting for you to come over. What took you so long?"

This trip had taken an interesting turn.

My eyes moved over her face. There was a déjà vu element about her, but I couldn't put my finger to it.

The staring must have been blatant as she uncomfortably fixed her sophisticated white wrap-dress. The outfit hugged the top half of her body and flared above her knees. The ensemble suited her—I grudgingly admitted— presenting up her tits like confection at a bakery and showing off a set of sexy as fuck legs.

Heat flared inside me, though my face remained stoic. I had no intention of making it easy for her. "You could have come up to me instead."

"And miss the chance to watch you intimidate that man?" She cocked her head at the creep slinking out of the bar.

She. Was. Savage.

The admiration I felt was enough to park my butt on the stool next to hers. "That was... fun," I conceded. "Do you want a drink?" I motioned for the bartender by raising my hand.

"That's an affirmative."

There it was again, recognition of having played this game before. Something about our conversation sounded rehearsed, but what was it?

The bartender interjected my gawking, eyeing the girl suspiciously.

In France, the legal age to consume wine was sixteen. Eighteen for hard liquor. Though most establishments didn't care, this was a tourist destination. A large demographic at this hotel consisted of American families. If those families found out that the hotel served hard liquor to their juvenile delinquents, it'd be a PR nightmare rather than a legal one.

"ID, please?" The bartender asked her in a thick French accent.

For the first time since laying eyes upon her, it dawned on me that she appeared young. Panic ensued on cue.

Fucking hell. What if I had been chatting up someone younger than eighteen?

My heart stopped when she reached inside her wallet to fish out her ID. She flashed it at the bartender—twenty-one.

Thank. Fuck.

I curiously studied the document as she put in a drink order.

Maya Mathews.

Libra.

Lived in Paris. Based on her accent, she was an ex-pat—an American who moved to France.

Blue eyes gleamed when she caught me snooping, and the déjà vu factor hit me like a hurricane.

The mischievous orbs on this girl held an uncanny resemblance to Mia.

* * *

"Mia, are you alright?"

"Yeah, I'm fine. Just looking for Milo." Mia peeked out from backstage, turning her head from left to right.

Mia was a kid genius/mad scientist—wicked smart, acutely observant, slightly eccentric, and spoke without a filter, though her statements were often valid. It was the reason I could tolerate her, despite disliking children as a general demographic. They were annoying, irrational, and incomprehensible.

But I never lumped Mia into that category. She came out of her mother's womb spewing adult lingo and acted like a grown-up.

Except for tonight.

Mia wrote a short story for a statewide competition, televised in front of a live audience. The prestige was lost on little Mia, terrified of being on stage and desperately hoping her family was in attendance—especially her brother, Milo.

"He's not here," she concluded, eyes glistening.

"He'll make it," I lied because I had a soft spot for Mia. Also, I hated being associated with any of Mia's negative experiences since our interactions were already limited.

Milo Sinclair might be my oldest friend and business partner, but he dubbed me a bad influence on Mia. If he weren't in a jam, I wouldn't even be here tonight as I constantly undermined his authority over Mia.

It was just so damn difficult to bite my tongue. Milo was a pseudo guardian to both of his younger siblings, but his expectations of them were insurmountable. Despite her paralyzing stage fright, he pushed Mia into this competition, only to be pulled away due to an emergency.

Mia's other brother, Reid, was caught purchasing alcohol with a fake ID and Milo had to deal with the fallout.

The auditorium roared with applause as they called Mia's name, further rattling her nerves. She shivered at the peril, and I desperately wanted to reassure her that she had the choice to walk away. But it wasn't my call to make... or was it?

"Do you think Milo will be mad if I don't read the story?" Mia asked in a small voice.

Yes. "Of course not."

"Really?"

My heart lurched at her saddened face, soul itching to console her. She was so fucking tiny, vulnerable, like a lamb to the slaughter. And those helpless, blue eyes—it was the ultimate guilt trip.

For God's sake, she was just a child, maybe ten or eleven years old, twelve at most. As the youngest Sinclair, Mia's needs were often sidelined by her family. She reminded me of a younger version of myself, a pang of camaraderie sparking at the bitter feelings I used to harbor for being an afterthought.

"Mia, it's your call. If you don't want to do this, you don't have to."

Mia wrung her wrists, twisting them in a continuous motion. "Milo's going to be pissed," she whispered unsurely.

"Forget about Milo. This is about you." Blue eyes looked up doubtfully as if the idea was unfathomable. "I think you might regret it if you don't go out there, but this is your choice. If you don't want to do it, we can leave."

Mia hesitated, contemplating the fallout with her brother.

I patiently awaited her response, but Mia seemed unable to pull the trigger. Closing my eyes, I provided an alternate solution. "Mia, if you like, we can tell them you aren't feeling well enough to read, and I can be your proxy."

"Proxy?"

"Your substitute. I'll read the story for you."

Her shoulders sagged. "They won't let us. We are supposed to read it ourselves so they can score our presentation as well as writing skills."

I grinned, tapping her nose. "You leave that to me, little Bunny."

She finally perked up, making my heart tug in my ribcage. I seized Mia's notebook and led the way from backstage to the platform with a spotlight and mic stand in the middle. A large auditorium filled with parents and teachers awaited her arrival, as did the television crew. The audience frowned at my on-stage presence while the cameramen wore bewildered looks as I took the mic.

"Hi everyone. My name is Brandon Cooper. I'm here to introduce an exceptional young lady, Mia Sinclair." I smiled, pointing at her. "Ms. Sinclair was extremely excited to share her story with you. Unfortunately, she came down with a case of tonsillitis, so I'll be reading this piece of art on her behalf."

Without missing a beat, I opened her notebook and proceeded. Half the struggle with breaking the rules was in the way you carried yourself. No one objected to the blatant disregard of policies if you acted confidently.

I had no idea of the words on the page, simply stampeding over and reading in an animated tone. It forced a giggle out of Mia, her nerves subsiding, as she stood with her back to the bewildered audience.

Our inspirational story of facing your fears wouldn't win Mia the competition. The core requirement was to present the story, not hire a grown man to make looney tune voices. However, something better transpired. By the time I finished, Mia was all but hackling on stage.

She had never graced a stage before without bursting into tears.

Tonight, Mia cured her intense fear of a live audience. Her face lit up like a Christmas tree as the realization dawned on her. Glossy eyes stared at me like I was some sort of savior. Her hero.

I couldn't recall the last time anyone regarded me as such. Who would have thought that Brandon Cooper, of all people, could be anyone's hero?

Luckily, I didn't have to worry about setting any expectations with that title, as the relish was short-lived.

"Brandon!" Milo strode purposefully through the lobby, shooting daggers at me with his eyes. All three Sinclairs had hot tempers. Milo was normally level-headed, but fury lurked behind his cold expression tonight.

I frowned. "Hey, man. What's going on—"

"What's wrong with you?" he asked stoically without any emotion.

What the hell. "Umm... I think you misspoke a few words there. You said, what's wrong with you, but you meant to say, I'm eternally grateful that you took care of my little sister tonight. But it's okay. Let's call it semantics."

"I caught the tail end of what was supposed to be my sister's big night. I should have never trusted you with Mia," he said coolly.

I leaned back, surprised. I truly acted with sensibility tonight, so what the fuck was his problem? "Dude, I gave up my night to hang out with your sister. Do you know how much I detest kids?" Though Mia was alright for a kid, I wouldn't admit it to Milo. Not while he was acting like an ass. "Is this how you thank me?"

"Thank you for what?" Milo's mien was incredulous. "I asked you to take my sister to present the short story she wrote. Guess what? She didn't recite it."

"Because she got stage fright and didn't want to do it. I read her essay so at least Mia could see that public speaking was nothing to be afraid of."

Milo scowled. "If I let Mia give up every time she didn't want to do something, she'd quit school and live off pop tarts. Kids don't get to make those decisions. As the adult, you were supposed to make a better decision on her behalf. At the very least, you could have called me first to check."

Did this guy ever take a day off?

Milo was infamous for lecturing Reid and Mia. He even held monthly lectures to go over the highlights from his past lectures.

He was exhausting!

"If you didn't like the way I handled things, then you should have been here yourself," I snapped, irritation nagging at me. "Mia was scared shitless when she realized you weren't there. What did you expect me to do?"

Milo stilled, his face ridden with guilt. But I didn't care.

Fuck him.

I was annoyed on Mia's behalf. The kid only entered this competition to appease Milo, and he was nowhere in sight when she needed him most.

Milo closed his eyes. "Brandon, I appreciate you looking out for Mia, but I enrolled her in toastmasters in preparation for this competition. You let her give up without even trying."

"Come on, man. How can you possibly be angry after I came through for you tonight?"

"And how many times have I come through for you?"

Touché.

I shouldn't have played that card. My mom passed away a few years ago. The only reason I got through her death was because Milo and Asher—my two best friends—refused to leave me alone.

I still tried to make him understand my point of view one last time. "Just one competition, man. It's not a big deal."

"Maybe for you. For Mia, this was a real opportunity." He sounded factual, not angry. "She has been dying to go to this summer camp for gifted children. If she had just read the story like we practiced, she would have won, and it would have guaranteed her a spot. But she was disqualified for having someone else read her work, and now I get to be the bearer of bad news."

"I didn't know," I muttered as he laid it on thick. I thought Mia was doing this to impress Milo, not because she wanted more for herself.

"You didn't care to know because everything is a joke to you. Hardships and struggles in life are of no concern. You'll always be filthy rich, but the rest of us don't get a pass."

Milo was wrong in insinuating that I had a free pass. My father was rich, but since Mom's death, I refused his financial help and was adamant about paying him back every cent he had ever spent on me.

However, I didn't contend the accusation. Not after costing Mia something she sought after.

"Brandon, I don't understand why you constantly contradict me about Mia. But I assumed that when push came to shove, I could count on you."

"You can."

"No, I can't. What you did tonight... you crossed a line, man." His face dripped with disappointment. "From now on, I don't want you anywhere near my sister. Mia is brilliant, and she is meant for bigger things. All of her teachers agree. We are supposed to help Mia reach her full potential. I don't need you filling her head about sailing through life like it's a breeze."

That. Poor. Kid.

She was the most brilliant tiny human, but it was clear she'd be forced down a path riddled with unrealistic expectations.

However, I kept my trap shut because I was the one at fault. It was Milo's call about how she was to be raised.

Mia chose that exact second to spill out of the auditorium exit. The light behind her eyes faded upon sensing the tension in the air. "Did something happen?" She looked back and forth between Milo and me. "Milo," she prodded, "are you mad that I didn't read the story?"

"No, Rabbit." Milo attempted to smile. "I'm not mad at you," he said pointedly, glare returning in my direction.

Mia was much too observant and knew I was taking the heat for tonight. Part of me—an irrational part—wished she would disclose my help conquering her stage fright.

I lived a life without expectations and forgot the exhilaration in impacting someone positively. Curious that such a simple thing—a child's smile—could give life meaning, truly outlining the hollowness of my otherwise lonely existence. And that minutely invigorating triumph was being snatched away.

It was unreasonable to expect a child to defy their parental figure at your behest, but an absurd side of me wished she'd verbalize the positive difference I had made. A reassurance that I wasn't the fuck-up Milo pegged me out to be.

Mia remained silent. No idea why that hurt the most.

Perhaps this fleeting disappointment was for the best. Clearly, my sympathy wasn't benefiting her, so there was no point in wasting my time.

Moving forward, my head needed to remain sharp and focused on my business relationship with Milo instead. At the age of twenty-two, I didn't have another faster ticket to financial freedom. Milo was the majority shareholder of our company, and pissing him off by meddling in his family affairs was the sure way to create a toxic workplace environment.

"I'm leaving." I glared at Milo, resentment reverberating through me. "Good night," I said to no one in particular.

Mia silently accused me of abandoning her at the lion's den. The hurt radiated from her—similar to the one I had felt at her silence—invoked by my cold demeanor. I still forced myself to stroll out of the lobby without a backward glance.

Sorry, kiddo! This is goodbye.

Brandon

MIA HAD BEEN LURKING in the back of my mind ever since I spoke to Milo, and he had mentioned her in passing. That little prodigy had an active brain prone to frequent outbursts. But was that really surprising? Unrealistic expectations had a way of consuming your soul from the inside out. Any kid would spiral if faced with pressures of such magnitude and left to deal with it by their lonesome self.

The thought triggered my sympathy for her all over again.

My guilty conscience for leaving Mia at the lion's den was fabricating a similarity between this Maya Mathews. And this woman's striking resemblance to Mia—a possible figment of my imagination—only proved to be disturbing.

Mia was just a child, and I didn't want her to be associated with someone I found attractive.

"Maya..." I drawled. "Did you just get into town?"

With a wicked grin, she grabbed the drink from the bartender. "Nope. We got here a few days ago."

We? "Oh. Are you enjoying your visit so far?"

She unsurely lifted a shoulder. "I'm not a big fan of the beach, but it's cool to be here with my friends."

"I have never met someone who dislikes the beach."

"The concept of sitting on a hot, sandy beach does nothing for me. I'm too ADD for that." She giggled. Not a muffled laugh with a hand over your mouth, as was commonly practiced by most women, but a real giggle.

Something inside my chest twisted at the sound. It was suffocating and liberating, all mixed in one.

"Do *you* like the beach?" she asked.

"Sure. But I miss the stimulation of a big city whenever I'm at the beach for too long."

"Hmm. I live in a big city but spend most of my stimulating time inside a research lab."

"Oh yeah? Are you about to cure cancer?"

"I wish. I work at a research lab for social sciences. It serves no purpose and is draining the college's resources. The Dean is looking into shutting it down, not that I blame him. Honestly, if I weren't desperate to get away from my crazy family, I wouldn't work there."

I laughed at her candor in front of a perfect stranger. "Everyone thinks their family is crazy. I'm sure they aren't so bad."

Any hint of playfulness abruptly disappeared, replaced by a grave look. "They are," she asserted, speaking as if questioning her opinion on the matter was detestable.

It was evident that I struck a nerve. She was offended by the comment, perceiving it as dismissive of her feelings.

Once more, this girl reminded me of little Mia, distressed by her family life. She had a particularly complicated relationship with Milo, imprinting on him like a baby bird ever since her birth.

As soon as the thought crossed my mind, I chided myself. Mia was supposed to be a useless topic. The last time I opened that pandora's box, it prompted Milo's wrath for meddling.

We were different; Milo was the responsible type while I was laid-back. Though he accepted those traits in a friend, it wasn't good enough of an influence on his beloved baby sister. And family was Milo's kryptonite, the rules regarding them non-negotiable.

I vowed to put a lid on it, ascertaining that the similarities to Mia ended with the gleaming eyes, blonde hair, and unhappy homes. Moving forward, I merely needed to refrain from personal speculations.

God, this was a lot of work, even for one lousy drink at the bar.

Sensing the tension, Maya changed the topic to something more amusing. "I feel like every girl here is checking you out."

Her eyes swept the room. I trekked after her eyes to find Farah and Tasha looking sideways. A lone figure at the bar stole glances in our direction, too. Along with a couple of women at the far corner as well. A group of girls at a nearby table. Possibly even one or two of the female servers.

"Can you blame them for staring?" I quirked an eyebrow.

Yes, I was aware of the effect I had on females. They went on about my "icy pale" blue eyes, 6'3 frame, and the impeccable physique I forced myself to keep up. But very seldom did an encounter worth mentioning occur.

A few determining factors resulted in my overly picky nature. Mostly, I didn't need the reputation of being a womanizer. Already had one for being an asshole.

Not to mention, women rarely piqued my interest. Even for a one-night stand, I had several criteria. Once taken into account, all of it drastically scaled the pool. I didn't relish dealing with drama, nor did I care for boring women without personalities. I also didn't like girls my age or younger, preferring the company of mature women. I hated girls with attachment to social media and particularly detested "selfies."

My standards for physical appearance were even more stringent, hardly identifying a woman as attractive. Hence, I was shocked to find myself attracted to this woman at first glance, possessed by an unknown quality.

“Haha, very funny.” She rolled her eyes. “Anyways, what brings you to Nice?”

"The convention, obviously." I paused, concealing the real reason for my visit. Most people were uncomfortable with morbid discussions. Although Maya didn’t strike me for most people, I was in no headspace to divulge.

Instead, I shifted our conversation to more neutral topics like religion, politics, and the middle east.

The inauspicious theme didn’t deter Maya, who passionately argued with me over politics and theology, giving me an unobstructed view of her scholarly mind. More astonishing was her ability to redirect the exchange to safer territories.

"What kind of music do you like?"

“You first.”

"Nineties all the way." Maya made a sweeping hand motion.

"Nineties was the last decade to produce good music. I feel like an old man who is always screaming: *what are you damn kids listening to, you call that music?*"

"Ugh! I know what you mean. Everyone only listens to House nowadays."

"Right!" I threw up both of my arms.

"It's not music!" we declared in unison, then froze.

College students were supposed to loathe nineties music. Generally, twenty-one-year-olds preferred Electronic or Trance. But Maya didn’t fit the mold because she was her own genre.

I watched her, somewhere between enthralled and suspicious about the too-good-to-be-true personality.

The unashamed gawking turned her coy, and she nervously sipped on her drink. My eyes inadvertently landed on her mouth as a droplet lingered behind. Without meaning to do so, I reached out to wipe it off with the pad of my thumb.

I audibly exhaled at the slight contact, the inexplicable sound drowned out by the noise surrounding us. Electricity shot through my system as if waking me up for the first time in my life.

Maya followed my thumb with her pupils.

She feels it too.

“One more drink?” I murmured when she polished off the remnants.

“Umm—” She looked down at the empty glass unsurely before hitting the lock screen of her phone to check the time.

She didn’t have the chance to answer as the bartender decided on her behalf. "Last call!"

“Last call? It’s not even midnight,” I argued.

Maya sighed. “That’s alright. I should get going anyways. I’m actually Cinderella, and my chariot is about to turn into a pumpkin.”

Unamused by her lousy joke, I grudgingly handed my card to the bartender, waving Maya off when she reached into her purse. Perhaps it was for the best if I resumed the original plans I put in place for the evening—drink myself into oblivion in my room.

“Stay for one more drink,” I uttered idiotically instead of saying goodnight.

"I don’t think anywhere else is serving alcohol at this hour."

We weren't in New York, and this particular area in Nice wasn't vibrant after midnight. Even the hotel nightclub closed at 1:00 a.m.

Pathetic.

Oh well. I needn’t do anything other than part ways with this girl. Time to send her packing. "Do you want to come back to my room for a drink?"

Maya blinked, processing my request.

I never invited girls back to my place during work events. *Ever.*

This night had clearly short-circuited my brain. That’s the only reason I was making such callous suggestions.

"As you mentioned, there isn’t anywhere else we can get a drink,” I pressed. “And I’m not ready to call it a night."

She glanced at her phone again. "Sure, I can stay for one more drink."

Masking the unexpected relief, I circled the bar to retrieve my card from the bartender, feeling impatient as Maya had implied a time constraint. The girl I met earlier in the night, Farah, walked up to the bar simultaneously. She grazed my arm in her effort to place a signed copy of her receipt on the counter. "Hello again, Brandon."

"Hello, Farah."

"I hope you aren't calling it a night already?"

Twisting my head, I kept my eyes trained on Maya. For the last thirty minutes, my attention had been locked on her lips.

"I asked if you were calling it a night?" Farah inquired, irritated.

With great effort, I dragged my attention back to her. "Unfortunately."

Farah would fit the bill for any man—pretty, brunette, tight dress—but did nothing for me. She must have been new to the industry. Otherwise, she would have known to save her efforts. My selective nature for females was no secret, and I planned to keep it that way.

"That's too bad. It's not quite my bedtime, and I was hoping to find people who were awake. Can you think of anyone?"

"Can't help you with that," I said pointedly, making eye contact with the bartender to signal for my card.

Farah followed my wavering gaze—which shifted back to Maya—and took the hint.

“Got it.” Farah knew when she had been bested and bowed out, cutting her losses with a knowing look. “Good night, Brandon.”

I nodded in acknowledgment. “Good night, Farah.”

“By the way,” she said over her shoulders, “my name is Tasha. Not Farah.”

It would have been an insult to both of our intelligence if I had apologized at that point. I didn’t care if her name was Tasha or Farah, and she knew it. For me, there were far more important things brewing.

I returned to Maya. "Ready?"
"Ready!"

Brandon

"AFTER YOU." Holding the door open with my outstretched arm, I invited Maya into the suite.

She whistled. "Nice room."

It wasn't. "I guess."

JAMBA, the app I built with my friends and christened with each of our first initials—Jaci, Asher, Milo, Brandon, Alexa—exceeded our expectations. It was a micro-investment app that rounded up change with every bank card transaction. A piggy bank for adults. The concept had been brilliantly received, and we enjoyed the fruits of our labor with a comfortable lifestyle.

However, Presidential Suites in Europe weren't held to the standards we were accustomed to. The room was spacious with a separate living room, balcony, and bar. Otherwise, there was nothing presidential about it.

I moved to the bar area, searching for a bottle of wine, hoping it would mitigate this foreign experience. I wasn't used to entertaining women, especially during work events.

Maya walked around the room, inspecting it. "What exactly does your job entail?" she awed, seemingly impressed by her surroundings.

Perhaps she was from humble beginnings and not used to the luxuries of life. Bypassing the cheaper wines, I uncorked the most expensive bottle on display and grabbed two glasses. "I manage the finances for our company."

"So, you're the money guy."

"Something like that." I handed her a wine glass with a generous pour.

"Cheers." She readily clinked our glasses, taking a long, slow sip. A silence enclosed on us for the first time tonight.

A maddening compulsion was reverberating through my pulse, making me act without reason. She had captured my attention from the moment she walked into the bar, causing me to bypass my rule about inviting a woman back to my place.

Though I was an otherwise reckless person, I protected one aspect with zeal—my reputation surrounding women. There was no justification for these impetuous actions. I was simply intrigued to explore every obscure layer she had to offer.

I glanced at her over the rim of my glass. In an almost depraved way, I reached out, thumb lazily stroking her forearm to see if the initial spark was still present.

My racing heart and her raised hair under my pad answered the question. The circular motion held us captive, soothing my broken heart while she steadied her stance. Neither looked away, eyes warring to see who'd blink first.

Hastily, Maya broke the spell by gracing me with the most unforeseen confessions.

"I'm a virgin."

“Huh?”

“I've never had sex,” she confirmed. There wasn't any doubt in her voice, nor was she awkward about the statement. “I wanted to inform you in case you expected more," she spoke in a matter-of-fact tone, waving her hand amid the minuscule space separating us.

I arrogantly presumed to have graced a woman with the honor of entering my private quarters at long last, and she... just humbled me by putting me back in my place.

Maya wasn't here for sex.

The irony was so comical that I could only lead with humor. "Wait a minute." I cocked my head. "Did you think we were going to have sex?"

"Umm."

"That was presumptuous."

"I didn't mean it like that—"

"Eyes up here, please." I crooked my index finger, insinuating she was staring at my crotch. "I'm more than just a hot body."

Maya burst out into a fit of laughter, the same one from before that had twisted up my insides.

"I know this must be really embarrassing for you because you're clearly obsessed with getting in my pants," I continued. "But I don't appreciate being objectified."

The pressure dispersed, leaving us with impish smiles. Hidden behind it was the mood-killing truth—Maya was a virgin, and I wasn't interested in inexperienced women.

"I should probably get going," she awkwardly fumbled. "I didn't realize it got so late."

Without thinking, I grabbed her elbow to stop her departure. The unintentional possessive act widened my eyes. Maya's gaze also landed on the hand gripping her tightly, though she remained unphased.

I needed to remove my grasp. If we couldn't fuck, there was no point further torturing one another.

"No way. I just opened this wine bottle. I'm sure the hotel will charge me an asinine amount for it. You can at least help me finish it."

She appeared unsure; perhaps the realization had dawned on her that an invitation to a hotel suite generally led to sex.

"Don't worry, I'm not in the business of stealing the innocence of impressionable young women. But we can have drinks... as friends. And you can tell me why men repulse you."

She huffed. "Being a virgin doesn't mean that I'm repulsed by men."

"Are you part of a sexless cult then?"

Her smile broadened.

"Religion?"

Maya shook her head.

"So, you're telling me that a beautiful girl willingly foregoes life's greatest pleasure for no particular reason? Blink twice if your pastor is listening to this conversation right now."

Maya blushed furiously, ears burning. "The concept that all religious people wait for marriage is archaic. Can we be done with this topic now and talk about you instead?"

"Me? I'm definitely waiting until marriage. Can't wait to have sex; hope it's fun."

Maya giggled, generating real magic in the air. "I meant, if we are discussing my sex life, yours should also be on the table."

I shrugged. "I'm an open book. I'll tell you everything. For starters, I'm not into virgins."

"Never?"

"Not even during my first time." I had no patience to teach the fundamental skills in bed. "It's too much work, and they usually have specific reasons for waiting."

Maya narrowed her eyes.

"Tell me I'm wrong."

"I'm not waiting for any specific reasons, per se."

"But you do have expectations for your first time."

"I don't want to have any regrets." She plopped her butt down on the couch, wine in hand. "And maybe I won't if it's with the right man, someone even my crazy family might approve of."

Then why did you come up to my room? I couldn't help but wonder. Sex was a given when going back to someone's hotel room. Did she really assume "a drink" truly meant a drink?

This girl was either naïve or overly optimistic about people's intentions. She never expected others to behave in an unsuitable manner because clearly Maya was sheltered. Explicitly, a good girl.

Strangely, she ended up in the lairs of the worst man.

"Did I overshare by telling you of my sexual status?" she asked unexpectedly.

With a deep sigh, I slid next to her on the couch. "I only came to this convention so I could scatter my dad's ashes in Europe. He passed away a few days ago."

The reason I needed to drown in alcohol. Being in Europe brought back memories, and the suffering had hit the hardest tonight.

"I'm so sorry, Brandon," Maya replied without missing a beat, not a trace of shock in her voice. Typically, the news of death brought on some form of outcry.

Maya was... unusual.

Oddly, her lack of reaction was the first appropriate one I had received. It was more comforting than hollow hysterics.

I forced a smile. "*That* was an example of oversharing. So, no. You didn't overshare."

Ignoring my false bravado, she asked gently, "Are you alright?"

I shrugged. "We weren't that close."

"Still, he was your father," she whispered. "No matter the relationship, loss is difficult."

I swallowed several times as the words rang true in my ears.

"We don't have to talk about this if you don't want to." Maya frowned, concern etched on her face.

"This conversation is just a little heavy." God, could we talk about anything else? Give me some motherfucking reprieve from these thoughts, please.

She picked up on the cue. "How about I lighten the mood with a joke?" I smiled at her effort. "What's the difference between a pregnant woman and a lightbulb?"

"What?"

"You can unscrew a lightbulb."

I almost spat out my drink. "Alright. No more talking about our families and no more bad jokes for the rest of our time together."

"It wasn't a bad joke. That was a classic."

"Classically bad."

She threw her head back to laugh—pure, unadulterated, and without restraint. I didn't have a camera, but I must have captured infinite mental pictures of her beaming face at that moment.

Suddenly, I felt grateful sex was off the table with her. With my history, this encounter would've turned sour, and I didn't want to be haunted by the ghosts of more people I hurt.

If we were to have the perfect sexless night and parted ways on good terms, I'd succeed in preserving the image of a picture-perfect girl in my mind. I'd safeguard it inside my brain forever, and on the gloomiest of days, I'd pull out this stolen moment for respite.

With the resolution to be "just friends," I attempted to keep my distance throughout the night, though Maya turned the modest task into the undertaking of the century.

"This scar is from track." She pushed up her dress to give me a peek of the silky skin on her upper thigh. The flesh taunted me, and I had to pinch my thigh to refrain from the urge to lunge at her. I hadn't taken her body into account during my earlier verdict that Maya was an ordinary beauty. Nor had I inspected her flawless skin or accidentally inhaled whiffs of her perfume.

"Did you fall?" I managed to rasp out with excessive difficulty.

"Yup. Right on the concrete. To make it worse, the girls behind me ran into me."

"Shit, they could have trampled you," I tsked in a displeased tone.

"I'm tougher than I look."

For the better half of the last hour, we had been trading scar origin stories, alternating between endless conversations on the couch and raiding the mini-fridge. The wine bottle was empty now, and the coffee table was filled with wrappers from our last snack ransack.

This evening wasn't what I envisioned.

It was better.

Though Maya sported slightly unconventional mannerisms, a trait dominant in those with less social experience, we established an unexpected bond. And despite the murky waters we treaded, it was clear that Maya was an optimist.

Maya entertained heaviness without letting it affect her idealism. She believed in science, though it didn't dissuade her faith in God—she wasn't a religious fanatic but held her convictions to profound esteem. The endearing dreamer side of her starkly contrasted with her otherwise controlled personality.

As the hours trudged along, I couldn't help but wonder what it would be like to experience the world through her mind—cognizant of the gloomy world we lived in yet refusing to allow the melancholy to take hold of your personality.

By the time it was dawn, there were no more pretenses left. I couldn't have survived the worst evening of my life without this tantalizing vision in front of me. She had successfully kept my mind off depressing shit throughout all hours of the night.

"Will you be around later today?" I asked out of the blue.

"Unfortunately, no. It was our last night here. I'm flying back to Paris," she regretfully informed.

"Oh." I barely knew her, and she meant nothing to me... so, why did I feel so fucked to hear that she was leaving?

"What are *your* plans?" She tucked a few stray hairs behind her ears.

It was hard to remain engaged after the bomb she had dropped. "I might drive to my dad's cottage in Italy," I ultimately professed, distracted by the thought of never seeing her again. "It's in this remote village, a few hours from here. We used to vacation there when I was young."

"Are you going to spread his ashes there?"

I nodded. Dad's cottage was the last place we shared a good memory. "Come with me." As soon as the words slipped out, my mind blanked.

"What?"

"Don't get on that flight. Come to Italy with me instead for the weekend."

She didn't respond.

Had I truly gone mad?

Most men enticed females with jewelry or dinner. I used a morbid rendezvous as bait. A funeral was meant to coax her into missing a flight.

"You want me there while spreading your dad's ashes?"

No. It was an impulsive suggestion. We had only just met; there was no way she was accompanying me to something so personal.

"Yes. We'll come back in a few days and then fly out together." The speedy proposal made me wonder if the plan was subconsciously brewing in the back of my mind all night.

Maya seemed uncertain. She was struggling with inner turmoil—her sympathy over my situation versus investing a whole weekend into a man whose romantic goals didn't align with hers, on the account that I didn't have any.

It was apparent she had whimsical notions. Maya might be a little geeky, but that didn't dissuade men. Even plain beauties like herself received plenty of offers for sex, last night being a case in point. Her choice to remain a virgin signified romantic fantasies.

"I hope we are friends at this point, and friends are supposed to help each other out, right?" I said to soothe her contemplations.

"And you don't have to worry about the cost. I'll pay for everything, along with your plane ticket."

Piercing blue orbs seared into mine, trying to read my impassive expression. "You don't have to do that," she whispered. "My ticket is changeable, but Brandon, this trip is personal. Are you sure you want me there?"

Like hell, she was right; this trip was goddamn personal. I didn't need anyone holding my hand while I spread daddy dearest's ashes. "I'd like that more than anything."

It was official.

I had gone certifiably insane.

Chapter 4

Brandon

AT THE CRACK OF DAWN, I fell asleep on the couch. Unbeknownst to me, Maya slipped out to grab her things. By the time my alarm went off, a neatly packed suitcase was waiting by the door.

The day turned out nothing like the one I had planned—strolling hungover while grumbling at my excessive drinking. Instead, I woke up sober, had breakfast in-suite with Maya, then grabbed my rental car to make a grocery run since Dad's cottage was far too isolated for restaurants. All the while, an efficient Maya rebooked her flight.

Maya was a glitch in the road map. Dad's ghost was punishing me with this girl; I was sure of it. Because this thing between us, it was a ticking time bomb waiting to explode.

We were to part ways on Tuesday, following the long weekend. It was already Saturday, leaving three more measly days with her.

By asking her to scatter these ashes with me, all I had done was prolong an inevitable goodbye. Yet, this overwhelming need for her had chased away my sensibility.

She is nothing but a reprieve from my guilt, I repeated in my head over and over as the car slogged up the hilly road. *She is not even that pretty.*

Unaware of the way she had turned my weekend upside down, Maya slumbered peacefully in my passenger seat. We stayed up all night and spent the day gallivanting between France and Italy. It was only two p.m. in the afternoon, but the sleeplessness had caught up. She was out like a light.

Hours, it seemed that I watched her, barely glancing at the empty road. Unable to fight back the urge, I traced my finger along her cheek, moving a few strands of hair out of the way for a better visual.

My pulse throbbed at the touch of her soft skin… God, this was frustrating.

She was in a blue-green summer dress with thin shoulder straps, long enough to reach past her ankles. It was no less striking than yesterday's dress, but the attire wasn't user-friendly.

Her teeth chattered even after I turned off the air conditioning. Girls were always cold. Did their minds live on a parallel hemisphere to convince their bodies of an imaginary temperature drop?

Maya curled up to her side into a small ball, arms tightly wrapped around her chest. The sight of her was vulnerable, like a kicked puppy in need of help. Blowing out a heavy breath, I reached back blindly, searching inside my duffel bag on the backseat. No hoodies turned up against my fingertips.

"Damnit," I muttered to myself.

Grabbing a handful of clothes instead, I dumped the pile on her, unfolding them clumsily to drape her with a makeshift blanket. The goosebumps on her arms stood to attention, and I ran my palm over it, rubbing until her skin heated up.

Once more, I felt her soft, heated… I nearly lost my coordination when Maya stirred.

"Are we there yet?"

I smirked. "Almost."

"What are you smiling at?" She yawned, stretching like a cat.

"You." I grinned ear to ear. "You sound like an impatient child."

"I'm not a child," Maya mumbled under her breath, sounding cross. She didn't recognize the compliment hidden behind my smile.

Last night, Maya's feral mind left me stunned as she explained Quantum Mechanics or spoke of civil unrest in Myanmar. I was in awe of her vivid optimism when she discussed her relationship with God.

Very rarely did she let her guard down throughout the night. But whenever I took a jab at her, she revealed snippets of a carefree personality, eyes sparkling lively. Her serious side was conjoined with goofy, spirited characteristics.

While the intellectual debates were thought-provoking, the instances she acted without restraint were my favorite. Her child-like persona had my head barely floating above water.

Ironic. The person to detest all child-like traits was now fumbling like a fool over the heartwarming effects of innocence. No, I wasn't referring to her intact hymen, but the way she eagerly hoped for the best, with enthusiasm and optimism.

It was so damn sweet.

The accolade was lost on a groggy Maya, sorting through the heaps of clothes covering her. "What's all this?"

"I thought you'd look nice in my clothing." I shrugged, hiding my amusement.

Maya rifled through the fabric, holding a shirt up by one edge. "Aww, you didn't want me to get cold." She didn't miss much, did she? "That's so cute," she teased as I deflected.

"It's cute that I covered you with my dirty laundry? Not even the high-ticket items; those are generic brands—buy two, get two for free at Walmart. I wouldn't read too much into it."

"I'm not reading too much into it. You are obviously head over heels in love with me."

I bit down on a sardonic smile.

"This is embarrassing for you since you are like obsessed with me now, but I'm a busy woman. It's not going to work out."

"And I was so looking forward to joining that sexless cult of yours."

I expected another retort. Instead, Maya shouted, "Watch out!"

The car screeched to a halt on the side of the road. "What the hell!" I startled.

"You just ran a red light."

We were at a T intersection. There hadn't been any cars around for miles, so I took a left turn at the red light. It was a typical action for these parts of the country.

Unable to understand the hysteria over such a trivial matter, I said, "Everyone runs through the traffic lights here if there are no other cars around."

She huffed, annoyed. "Are you crazy? Who does that?"

"It's not that big of a deal. Chill."

"I won't *chill*," she air quoted the word. "You could have killed us."

I barely suppressed the urge to roll my eyes. "You are being really dramatic."

"And you are being a reckless driver."

"I'm not." I shifted the gear back to drive. "We haven't even seen another car in miles."

"That doesn't matter. Rules are there for a reason."

The tension was thick in the air, but my curiosity was piqued. "Do you always follow the rules even if no one's watching?"

Maya blinked. "What do you mean?"

I tapped my lips in the deliberation of rules that were socially acceptable to break. "Have you ever gone to a café and used the Wi-Fi without buying anything?"

"Of course not. That's stealing."

"Been in a car without a seatbelt?"

"That's super unsafe."

"Okay. How about jaywalking, given there were no cars around?"

She looked out the window, her silence enough of a reply.

Jesus. This girl hadn't lived a day in her life.

"Rules and principles add structure to our lives, but that doesn't mean you still can't live it to the fullest," she finally replied, reading my thoughts.

"So, you never question authority or why they put a rule in place?"

"Not really."

"Following the rules is the reason for the worst crimes in the world. It's the people with blind faith in authority who butcher masses and start wars. There is nothing wrong with questioning the rules because the people to put them in place don't always know what's best."

She didn't comment but weighed my words while I did the same with hers.

At the next red light, I came to a complete stop. I only pulled away after the light turned green. Maya finally turned her head in my direction and... smiled.

Minutes passed before I glanced at the rearview mirror to find a foreign expression. The pure happiness written on my face was so eerie that I pondered if it was a reflection of another man.

All from one damn smile.

What the hell was happening here?

"There it is." I pointed in the distance ahead.

The seemingly endless road closed in on our destination. We watched the cottage grow larger with our impending approach, a stone pathway leading us into the house.

Unruly trees and branches hovered over to add a tropical ambiance though I had presumed Dad would have changed the landscape by now.

I parked on the paved driveway, then grabbed my duffel and

Maya's suitcase. She scrounged for the grocery bags, following me to the front door.

After a momentary pause, I punched a sequence of numbers into the lock pad. The door opened, shocking me. I was prepared to call my family lawyer for the new combination, but it turned out that Dad had never changed the code either—my birthday.

James Cooper was a good father before his mid-life crisis. One day, he unceremoniously dumped my mother after knocking up a woman half his age. He started drifting into the background of my life until the day I found myself searching for Dad's face during my basketball games. The way he faded out of our lives, I never expected such a sentimental gesture.

More peculiar was the interior of the home. It took several minutes to process the surroundings, a house preserved in time.

The open floor plan revealed textured wood cabinets in the kitchen with a granite countertop island. Log walls covered the living room with a chandelier dropping down the middle. The bedrooms were adorned with similar decorations, my handiwork.

My Dad's family was tremendously wealthy. I was an entitled prick with a blasé attitude, deferring to the family money to sail through life. However, Dad was adamant in training me the skill sets he deemed necessary for every man. He turned the house into a family project, teaching me to fix it up with my own hands. Our craftsmanship reflected Mom's taste—rustic mixed with modern elegance.

Dad never changed the renovations that summed up our family.

"It's beautiful," Maya offered, placing the grocery bags on the kitchen island.

Hit by the sudden nostalgia, I distractedly nodded, dropping the duffel bag and suitcase on the floor. "Mom picked out everything in this house, but I assumed my stepmother would have changed it by now."

Carmen had erased all traces of my mother, redesigning every property Dad owned. How in the hell did this place survive?

"I guess your father didn't let her."

"No, he didn't," I acknowledged.

Dad preserved this place to conserve his former life, even leaving the combination code untouched. The small piece of reassurance brought me an astonishing amount of peace. For so long, I had assumed we were nothing to Dad except his forgotten family, that I couldn't stop myself from reveling in the consolation.

Dad and I both moved on with our lives. Yet, we remained connected through this home in a parallel time and space. This cottage brought him solace, the way it did for me—a common denominator allowing us to reminisce and remember each other fondly.

"Dad left me this house," I said absentmindedly. "Actually, he left me with almost everything. The lawyer sent me his will, along with a letter to explain. I haven't even opened it."

"That's understandable. You had a complicated relationship with your father," she assessed, eyes full of compassion. I wondered if she'd show me such sympathy upon learning the whole truth.

I restlessly paced the living room. "We should go spread the ashes," I briskly muttered, overwhelmed by the new development. The weight in my heart dragged me heavily toward the center of the earth.

Maya paled at my abrupt tone, though she didn't contradict me. "Sure. Where do you want to do it?"

"There is a beach nearby," I garbled. "It was our favorite place." Until I unburdened myself of Dad's remnants, I wouldn't be myself again. I had to scatter those damn ashes, then shut down all emotionally taxing feelings.

I needed to run away.

Brandon

"SHOULD... should we say something to commemorate him?"

The evening breeze played with Maya's beachy-blonde hair. Paired with the blue of her eyes, she meshed well with the environment—the Mediterranean Sea and a sandy beach backdrop. However, it was her sea-green bohemian dress, long enough to dip into the water, that branded her as an extension of the ocean.

It was close to dusk, so the beach was deserted. There were no sailboats on the water either. Maya looked like the sole survivor on a remote island. The sight of her was calming during this dismal event. Peaceful and blue until a torrid shift turned her wild and unpredictable.

"Maybe a few words about his life," she suggested, ripping me out of my reverie.

Too choked up from the earlier discovery, nothing noteworthy about Dad's accomplishments came to mind. I merely stood with the urn in hand, ankle-deep in water.

"I'll give you a moment alone," she whispered when I failed to respond.

"No," I hurriedly protested. "Can... can you say something?"

"Me?"

"Yes." The peculiarity of the request wasn't lost on me, but... "Do you mind?"

"I-I didn't know him."

"Anything would do, really." I glanced at her, hoping she'd entertain my non-verbal plea. "It's the right thing to do, but I-I can't..." I couldn't finish the thought.

I didn't want to spew lies by saying only good things about Dad. I also didn't want to speak ill of the dead. Maya didn't know him. If she spoke positively about Dad, it wouldn't be a farce. It was appropriate in a weird way.

Maya examined me closely instead of expressing discomfort over giving a eulogy for a stranger. She had worn the same forlorn look during our short walk to the beach.

Maya was deep in thought, evidently organizing the words in her mind. Face charred with resolve, she cleared her throat to deliver a speech so eloquent that it left me stumped.

"We are here today to celebrate the life of James Cooper—husband, father, friend.

I didn't know him, but I do know his son. And if Brandon is any reflection, then James must have been a wonderful human being. Long after leaving this earth, his love will continue to shine through Brandon, a token of James' most meaningful contribution to this world.

With that solace, we'll remember James fondly, letting go of all memories filled with disappointment or hurt. With this goodbye, we heal all wounds, knowing this parting is temporary until you meet again to express all that was left unsaid during your time together.

Ashes to ashes, dust to dust, we commit James to earth for resurrection to eternal life."

I didn't dare bat an eyelid, worried that the illusion enunciating the words I needed to hear the most might disappear if I blinked rapidly.

Obviously, she was a figment of my imagination because the only way she could have read the words etched inside my heart so accurately—almost verbatim—was if I made her up. And if I conjured this consolation, I'd rather live inside the fantasy than go through this pain alone.

Hence, I measured my blinking.

Maya placed a hand on my bicep, contradicting physical reality against the mirage that might vanish. "Is there anything else you'd like to add?"

Since Dad's death, there was an urgency to unload for the first time. I shouldn't risk marring the perfect goodbye she had given me, but I also couldn't run away. Not after it had become apparent that Dad never erased me the way I did with him.

"I hated Dad for a long time because of Mom," I mumbled, voice barely distinct over the crashing waves. "She couldn't deal with it after Dad left us for another woman and spun out of control. She OD'd on painkillers my senior year of high school," I revealed.

Maya took a sharp inhale. "Brandon, I'm so sorry."

It was a deep, dark family secret that I never shared. We didn't talk about such things in our circle, though it was prevalent within New York City's elites. Everyone did drugs, cocaine, alcohol. Rehab was like a vacation to these people.

But Mom wasn't like them, truly. Sarah Cooper was the pillar of her community, president of various charitable foundations. And she was a good mother.

However, as Dad paraded around his new wife—a woman only a fraction of his age—the humiliation became unbearable. Mom was only trying to suppress the pain but miscalculated the dosage her tiny body could handle.

It was an accident.

I shook off the image of my mother during the latter years of her life—frail, skinny with thinning hair. "I was a mess when Mom died. Worse, I still had to live with Dad until graduation."

Maya noiselessly lingered, correctly presuming there was more to the story.

"I blamed him for everything and couldn't stand the sight of his new family. I barely spoke to my half-brother. Never attended family dinners. After moving out for college, I cut Dad out of my life entirely."

I paused.

Maya didn't push me. She knew the art of silence—one infrequently practiced by others— the skills to realize when a conversation didn't require words from both parties.

The truth was still hard to disclose.

Though I vilified Dad, he regretted our relationship and tried to fix things in later years.

After Mom's death, any interaction with Dad felt like a betrayal toward her. I wanted nothing more to do with him, hoping it would absolve me of the guilt. So, I stubbornly thwarted all of his efforts. To add insult to injury, I tracked all major expenses Dad had incurred on my behalf, saved up, then threw a check in his face.

For a time, I was smugly satisfied to achieve my petty goal. But with his final act on earth, Dad took away any satisfaction from my "win" and humbled me in the most profound of ways.

In his will, Dad left me with his entire inheritance.

"Our last communication was some texts he had sent, asking me to visit," I faintly uttered at long last, swallowing the lump growing in multiples. "I thought the messages were about his usual attempts to reconcile and ignored them. Didn't even open them. Didn't pick up the calls from my stepmother either. I had no idea he was in the hospital."

I gauged Maya's reaction over my trifling actions. She merely nodded, inaudibly encouraging me to rip off the Band-Aid to face what was lurking underneath.

"Dad died two days later," I concluded with the inevitable ending. Dad was fighting a losing battle after a car accident. He was texting and calling to make amends before his time expired. His last text would haunt me forever.

Please son, I just want to say goodbye.

"I have no one to blame but myself for never saying goodbye to my father." I avoided Maya's gaze, my face passive and cold. Was she appalled, horrified, sickened?

Shocking me, Maya hugged me. "He knew that you loved him," she whispered.

Did he, even though I was the son of a bitch who never visited his father on his deathbed?

"He knew that you loved him," she repeated. "And he loved you too. He didn't change the cottage because it reminded him of the good times with you. He loved you, Brandon."

Maya spoke with so much conviction it was difficult to deny the assertion. So, I remained silent, closing my eyes.

My heart was blackened beyond repair after Mom's death. Filled with resentment and blinded by anger, I couldn't forgive Dad. It only left me with regrets over my failure to rectify our broken bond when he died.

It was fucking poetic that the bi-annual convention was right around the corner because there was no place better suited to spread his ashes. Europe was special to our family, though I never expected the happy memories to haunt me.

The pain had multiplied by ten folds upon my return to this continent. On that fateful evening, I had been searching for salvation at the bottom of a glass when Maya arrived, saving me from the worst night of my life.

As it turned out, I didn't need salvation; I required absolution—delivered by *her*. I came to Europe for closure. Instead, I found something far more valuable.

I found *her* and finally, I wasn't so alone anymore.

With my eyes still closed, I let that warmth of hers spread through me, realizing that I never wanted it to end. How long had it been since someone hugged me or comforted me? Months? Years?

She had torn down every wall with one embrace, and I never wanted to put them back up. I could only hope that I wasn't alone in feeling this way, that there were two lonely souls on that beach, not one. Because this thing flowing between us, it was more than sympathy, more than superficial attraction, and a lot more intense than anything I had ever experienced.

Maya stepped out of my reach with an unspoken understanding of what had to come next. I had suffered, lost, grieved... and then I had found *her*. Now, that's all that mattered. It was time to put everything else to rest.

I tipped the urn, allowing the wind to take the course. For the first time in my miserable life, I prayed to God, hoping Maya's words were true. That I'd see Dad again to convey everything I never had the chance to say.

With this goodbye, we heal all wounds, knowing this parting is temporary until you meet again to express all that was left unsaid during your time together.

The last of the ashes soared aimlessly, taking with it all Dad had done wrong, leaving only the cherished memories behind.

With that solace, we'll remember James fondly, letting go of all memories filled with disappointment or hurt.

At long last, my cynical veil lifted, finally letting me see the world through Maya's optimistic eyes, and it was... perfect.

She was perfect.

Brandon

"ORANGES, EGGS, BREAD," Maya listed our food options for the weekend while I put away the groceries. "Oo, steaks and mushrooms." She grabbed the two items. "Can we have this for dinner? Please. It's my favorite."

"Sure." I smiled. A conditional promise, depending on the functionality of the grill. But I had no intention of dampening her spirit without exhausting all resources, not when she asked so sweetly.

"Yay! I'm so excited." She nudged her head toward the bulky, ancient television. "By the way, does that thing turn on?"

"It should. Our groundskeeper would have fixed it otherwise."

"Groundskeeper?"

I pointed at the white, rectangular device mounted on the kitchen wall, next to the stove. "You see that remote-control looking thing? If we ever need cleaning or something fixed around the house, we press the orange button to page our groundskeeper. But he still comes by regularly to maintain the property. He would have replaced the TV if it was broken."

"Perfect." Maya clapped her hands, practically glowing. "Then we can have a steak and movie night."

Steak and movie night.

Sounded an awful lot like a date... an intimate one after the necessary formal ones had concluded, and you were comfortable staying indoors on a Friday night.

I grilled the steaks over the next couple of hours and hunted down a stash of Dad's favorite red wine. As I set the table, my nerves flared. I hadn't engaged in the familiarity of eating at home with anyone in years.

However, my apprehension over the intimate date amounted to nothing. Maya barely ate two bites after laying out the dinner spread, sprouting she was full.

I wasn't interested in nourishment anyways, starving for an entirely different type of feast. My wandering eyes wouldn't stop roaming her body. A surreal peace had befallen me ever since we scattered the ashes, and I couldn't look away from the cause of it.

"How about that movie?" I murmured, moving us to the couch.

"Let's do it." She appeared visibly relieved by the suggestion.

Maya was nervous. Darkness had fallen outside, a reminder that we were staying overnight in a remote cottage. It was nerve-wracking for her, no doubt. The way my eyes were hungrily perusing every inch of her body didn't help the matter.

Averting my wandering gaze, I flipped through the channels absentmindedly, preoccupied with the skin accidentally brushing up against mine. We were sitting a hair's breadth apart. If I slanted my body, we'd be touching. My breathing accelerated in anticipation. I was so unfocused that I hadn't a clue what was on the screen.

Maya leaned forward to set her wine glass on the coffee table. Locks of golden hair cascaded down her creamy shoulders as she leaned over.

At that second, I determined an error in my judgment by categorizing Maya's physical attributes as ordinary. My measurement of her beauty was wholly incorrect because Maya was...

Drop.

Dead.

Gorgeous.

In fact, running through a mental inventory, I couldn't recollect meeting anyone in my lifetime to surpass the attraction I felt toward her.

Beauty was in the eyes of the beholder, and in my eyes, there was no one prettier.

The motif was hardly justifiable to explore more with someone from a different continent. But I could point out that I didn't appreciate her physical outlook—or even consider her particularly beautiful—a mere twenty-four hours ago. She only became the most beautiful woman on earth after my feelings had altered.

Hoping to understand the foreign emotions, I kept glancing at her, my attention fixated on her lips.

Generous.

Pouty.

Slightly pink.

I wondered if they tasted the way she smelled—roses and wildflowers.

So. Fucking. Enticing.

And I was... So. Fucked.

Maya dared to sporadically meet my glances while I dug my fingernails into the sofa fabric to release the sudden amplified ache. I was drowning in a heady fog, roaming mindlessly. The only guide out of this haze was her scent. It engulfed my lungs, making me lightheaded.

I pointed the remote at the television and watched it flicker. Maya stilled, unsure of why I had switched the box off. My arm wrapped around her waist to haul her onto my lap, draping her legs over my thighs.

"Brandon?"

I tilted my head, searching for the lips that had endlessly tormented me. Maya moved her face at the last second, my mouth landing on her neck instead.

Lips latched onto her skin as if searching for the meaning of life. Nose nudged between the crook for a deep inhale, the scent of her intoxicating.

My head was groggy, and my heart was beating so hard against my chest I feared it'd burst open any second. I shifted us rather clumsily without paying attention to the destination, savagely taking my fill as if there would never be enough time in the world to devour her.

“Brandon, I-I...”

Her ragged breath fanned my cheek. I was positive she shared a vital piece of information, but my ears were ringing from the adrenaline, eyes staring blankly in an abyss.

Where am I again?

"Brandon, wait," she pleaded.

The vulnerability laced in her tone made the hair on my neck stand out. It snapped me out of the stupor. Arduously, I ripped my mouth off her sweet-tasting skin.

It took several seconds to reclaim my ground and evoke my surroundings.

Things had escalated. Maya was pinned underneath me, dress bunched around her hips, my erection pressed against her groin.

I had lost control. Worse yet, I didn't care to regain it.

The girl had indeed drugged my mind.

“We should stop.” She pressed her forehead against my chest, voice thick with... disappointment? “It’s a bad idea to get so carried away over one weekend."

“I know our situation is complicated,” I rasped, the shuddering breaths a testament to what she was doing to me. “But we can figure this out. Returning to our lives doesn’t mean—"

“You told me yourself that you don’t do virgins,” she cut me off.

It was true.

I had vowed not to distort the image of this playful girl because even sleeping with me was a risk for fragile hearts. I was the sarcastic, unreliable guy—an asshole who ditched his prom date to get hammered with friends. The guy always leaving a trail of tears in his wake. In the past, I stood women up because I couldn't be bothered with the trouble of sitting through a lousy meal.

But it was different with her because… it just was.

"What I said, it's irrelevant now. It's not like that—"

"Brandon, it's okay." With a heavy sigh, Maya closed her eyes. "You don't have to explain yourself. I don't expect anything from you, and I certainly don't need to hear false promises."

Using my elbows as leverage, I slightly lifted myself.

Maya only gathered information about me during the microscopic time we spent together. So, the certainty in her tone struck a nerve. To barely give this a chance, to not even entertain the possibility it could work, seemed so… premeditated.

Sure, my past was nothing to boast about, but things could be different between us. After all, weren't all relationships a risk for heartbreak?

"Look, I understand your hesitation. All I'm saying is that this weekend doesn't have to be the end of it all."

"It does," she whispered. "If we don't stop, we'll both regret it."

My heart thundered as comprehension settled in.

Maya meant to say: *she* will regret it.

Maya was still a virgin at her age because she was the kind of girl who waited for the right guy to indulge in sex. She had already written me off before this conversation because she had high expectations… just not from me.

I don't expect anything from you.

The disheartening thought provoked my heart, beating madly under her palm. My body flared though my face remained placid.

Fuck. Her.

In what parallel universe was I not good enough for *her*. She would be so damn lucky. Was she blind to have missed the women eye-fucking me when we were out together?

I had every resource at my disposal, more money than she could ever dream of, I could have anyone I wanted. Yet, she'd rather save it for a fantasy man than give it up to *me*?

It was preposterous to envy an imaginary man, yet that's how it was. Jealousy sank its ugly claws into my soul at the thought of Maya searching for a man who'd fit the bill. The idea of her looking at him, letting him touch her... touch what's mine... oh hell!

"Ow!"

I bit hard at the base of her neck. An inappropriate show of aggression, a primal need to mark the girl I had no claim over.

Maya ground her jaw to suppress the reaction. "What the hell, Brandon!"

Placing my lips on her flushed skin, I licked the bruise with care. "I want you." My voice shook as I steadied my manic temper.

"I'm sorry," she groaned. "I can't do this!"

"And I can't think straight until I kiss you," I faintly whispered. It was absurd that I still hadn't tasted her lips.

She stared, eyes teeming with doubt.

"After all the shit that happened, you have no idea how much I need this." I hugged her close. "How much I need you," I added inaudibly.

"This isn't a good idea... it's not..." She grappled for words as I dragged my lips across her heated cheek, nearing my destination.

"Just let me kiss you," I spat out with difficulty, barely hanging on by a thread.

My lips loitered with an unrelenting lure until her reservation cracked. A part of me was convinced she needed to take that last leap of faith on her own.

Maya finally caved. "Just one kiss."

I pressed a kiss on the corner of her mouth before our lips met in perfect synchronicity. Slowly, possessively, I held her mouth hostage. My tongue moved leisurely against hers, the taste of her dominating my senses.

"You have no idea... how badly," I shuddered in between words, "I have wanted to do that."

My brain felt like it was made of cotton candy—fuzzy and weaved with the sweetness of this woman's aroma. Dragging her face closer, I kissed her again, pressing my body against hers. Several times, I opened my eyes to verify it was real.

She pushed against my chest. "Okay. That's it."

"Don't." I grabbed her wrists, trembling from spouts of desperation to taste her again. Pinning her hands on the sofa, I swooped down, this time without holding back.

My tongue lewdly tasted the bitter-sweet remnants of the red wine inside her mouth. Insatiably. Ferociously.

"We nd to stp," she spoke the muffled words against my mouth.

"Not yet." I couldn't fathom the idea of stopping. "Just... a little longer," I pleaded with an urgency I had never known before. Hands roamed freely, touching every part of her body, gliding the dress up her silky-smooth thighs.

"Wait," Maya protested weakly.

"Shh," I coaxed. "It's okay, baby."

Her eyes flew open, astonished.

It was my turn to freeze. I didn't practice words of affection or pet names during physical intimacy. It had slipped out, and honestly, it didn't feel forced, solely natural.

"I need to..." I struggled to verbalize, "...feel your skin."

I continued to lift her dress with care—stopping only to breathe in her scent—so she wouldn't notice I was unwrapping her like a precious Christmas gift. Nudging her legs wider, I rubbed against her groin, barely containing the urge to rip off the underwear and fuck her raw.

She pressed her thighs together. "Brandon, I told you... we can't have sex."

"Then let me make you feel good... if this is all we can have, at least let me touch you." I grazed my fingertips over her heated core. Liquid surfaced over the thin fabric of her underwear, making me groan.

This time, Maya stayed put.

I pulled at the hem of my shirt over my head, discarding it onto the floor. I reached for her dress next. Her tits sprung free as I lifted the dress over her chest with a quick maneuver.

Maya was stretched out under me, moving her face to the side, deflecting. She didn't want to bear witness to what we were doing in the dark. It was evident that no one had seen her naked before, and she was stuck somewhere between insecurity and hesitancy.

"Beautiful," I awed, squeezing her firm breasts, not letting her doubts rule the moment. "Unbelievably beautiful."

My hungry eyes raked her tight body with miles of smooth skin. A long neck with defined décolleté and a perky set of tits. She had the slightest dip on the sides of her flat stomach, giving her the right amount of curves. Her legs were toned and firm, just like the rest of her.

Perfection.

I couldn't wait any longer and dipped my hand under her thong to touch her bare, making circles around her clit. She shuddered, her thighs jerking uncontrollably.

Velvety moisture coated my fingers, ripping sweet moans out of Maya's mouth. "Oh, God."

I pushed a finger inside her, the heat welcoming me with open arms.

"Brandon, I—"

Her mouth hung open mid-sentence when I pressed my thumb on her clit, finger moving in and out of her tight hole. "That's it," I encouraged. "Don't overthink it. Just let me make you feel good."

Maya laid naked, writhing underneath, setting me ablaze with her reactions. Eyes closed, teeth sunk into her bottom lip, left leg hung limply off the couch with a foot resting on the floor.

I kissed down her trembling body toward the southern region, making a trail with my tongue. I only stopped at the taste of fabric—her thong. Licking through the thin scrap of material, I tasted the liquid that had surfaced.

It was more than what I could bear. I shoved the material down with force, my tongue landing on her pussy to lick the droplets pouring out freely.

"Holy shit!" Maya screamed at what I realized was an unfamiliar sensation for her.

I roughly spread her thighs wider. She was served up on a platter as I explored all of her. Sucking on her sweet clit, feeling her pussy pulse, the throbbing, the blood pumping at her most intimate spots.

Maya pushed her hips upward in an insatiable manner. She was breathless, restless, and begging for relief. Ready to explode.

"I'm... oh God!" Maya sounded bewildered, lost.

The pleasure drew out erotic sounds, driving me to the brink of insanity. I only stopped as her thighs quaked around my head when Maya reached her peak.

I shot forward, my mouth landing on her stiff nipple. My hand squeezed her breast as I sucked on the sensitive tip standing to attention, distracting Maya, who hadn't come down from her orgasm high. I shoved a second finger inside her, pressing in and out determinedly.

"You're so sexy," I gritted around her breast. "Do you have any idea what you do to me?" I demanded roughly, guiding her hand to my crotch to show her. The rock-hard bulge strained painfully against the lining of my jeans.

With caution, I unbuttoned my jeans to whip out my dick and forced her hand to wrap around it.

"Fuck," I hissed at the first touch.

Doused with lust, Maya didn't snatch her hand back. She stroked me out of pure instinct, dazed, unable to focus on the here and now.

The room filled with our heavy panting, the sounds bouncing off all corners of the walls. I removed her hand and grabbed my cock to rub it against her slick heat. Her eyes flew open to find the angry red veins sliding between her pussy lips.

"Brandon, what are you doing?" she panted.

"Just..." tremors from the control spiked my voice, "going to rub it against you."

"Brandon, don't—"

I rhythmically massaged her folds. "Don't ask me to stop. It feels too good. Fuck. I want to come with you. We don't have to go any further."

She didn't speak for several beats before whispering, "That's all you'll do?" The words were so faint I wondered if I misheard them.

"Yes," I whispered just as low, gratified for the sanction.

However, her next sentence put a damper on any elation. "Okay. That's all we'll do. And then we go back to our lives like this never happened."

My chest expanded, provoked by the same damn sentiment to elevate my anger in the first place. It made me want to punch my face so the pain would divert the sting in my heart.

I stroked her clit with my cock violently. Grabbing under her thigh, I raised it to her waist. I didn't let myself think as I removed the fingers inside her, spearing her tight, wet hole with my tip instead. Barely.

Maya pushed for distance once more. "Brandon, I told you that we can't—"

I kissed her, fingers reaching between us to caress her sensitive clit. My mouth, the fingers, all played her in perfect harmony, driving her mad, driving myself mad.

"Fuck." Maya arched off the couch, mouth parted as the crescendo built.

Inch by inch, I plunged my hips forward. She was drenched, but the resistance was still far greater than anything I had experienced before. Gritting my teeth, I moved with precision.

Maya whimpered from the foreign invasion. But every time her eyes threatened to flutter open, I drowned her with a variety of sensations to sidetrack her mind from what I was doing to her body. Time stood still as I pierced the narrow channel, breaching through to fill her.

"Holy shit," I panted. The wild beats of my heart boomed, and for a second, I might have even blacked out. She was...

Pure.

Fucking.

Bliss.

"You... feel... unbelievable." I bit down on her neck, juddering.

Her tight walls choked me, begging for me to fuck her harder, but her pained exhalations slowed my enthusiasm. I allowed Maya all the time to adjust, finally pulling back with measured control.

Maya became lucid, the physical pain overruling the other sensory overload. I paced myself to savor every second even as my muscles clenched from the restricted movements, my fingers on her clit matching the rhythm.

"Fuck, Maya," I moaned.

Her eyes flew open, filled with untamed fire and a wild thirst. Suddenly, Maya dug her nails into my shoulders hard enough to draw blood as her mouth met mine with equal savagery. Whether it was revenge for tricking her into sex or she was in the throttle of pleasure remained to be determined, though it pushed me over the edge.

The hammering in my ribcage went into overdrive. I plunged myself deeper, only to pull out seconds later as the most violent orgasm of my life took root, hitting me with wave after wave of pleasure. "Fuck!" I roared, cum splattering on her stomach.

My entire body went limp, and I melted into Maya before her

back could hit the sofa. Realizing I must be crushing her, I managed to shift my weight to the side, breathing heavily.

"That... you... it was..." I couldn't finish the thought. My panting turned the words into insoluble sounds. "I knew it... when we met. You were meant to be mine." It took minutes to formulate a sentence somewhat coherently.

She peeked up, looking so docile that I felt obliged to add a consolation comment regarding her virginity.

"It wouldn't have been this good with anyone else."

Despite her beguiling nature, Maya knew what I meant.

All her life, she waited for the right guy.

Too bad for him; she met the wrong guy first.

Brandon

LAST NIGHT, I expected Maya to be pissed—or at least reprimand me—for seducing her in the way I did. But Maya didn't voice any more objections throughout the night, remaining complacent when I dragged her back to my bed and buried my face between her legs until she passed out, delirious.

And for the second consecutive morning, I was immersed in Maya's warmth. My arm was banded around her. The soft body molded into me as if custom-built for the very purpose.

As sunlight streamed through the window, the light of day reflected a different reality for us—yet another day from our limited time together had expired.

I grabbed my sweatpants off the floor and headed to the bathroom, dreading the obscure future. After only a short time together, I couldn't process—nor could I remember—a time before Maya. She had staked a claim, marking herself so deep that it couldn't be eradicated.

Once this weekend perished, could she really return to her previous law-abiding life, chalking it off as a wild adventure?

The thought had me squeezing the tube of toothpaste with more force than necessary.

"Morning," Maya mumbled, lifting her head off the pillow. She rubbed her eyes and waited with uncertainty before dressing, searching through her bag that I had brought in earlier.

I glanced at her briefly, my expression neutral. Though it wasn't Maya's fault, I felt irrationally hostile. I needed her out of my sight. "Do you mind putting on a pot of coffee?"

"Sure." Maya twiddled her thumb at the edge of the bed. "How do I make coffee?"

"You've never made coffee before?" I gaped at her through the reflection of the bathroom mirror. "What do you do for coffee when you are at home?"

She lifted an unsure shoulder. "Walk to Starbucks."

Fucking adorable.

Surely, I was out of my wits for this woman because her ineptness cured my foul mood. I walked to the kitchen with a dramatic eye roll, though part of me was abnormally content with the information.

She needed me.

Maya was book smart, incredibly so. But it was evident that she had been shielded all her life, lacking the skill sets to perform the most menial tasks. In some ways, though microscopic, Maya needed me as much as I had come to need her.

I removed the coffee bean bag and put on a fresh pot while an inquisitive Maya shadowed my every move. She soon became distracted by her phone screen.

"My phone isn't working," she announced out of the blue.

"That's because there is no cell service around here. Price you pay for privacy."

"I know," she relented. "Even the Wi-Fi is down. I probably have to check in for my flight at the airport kiosk. What time are we driving back on Tuesday?"

A piercing pain stabbed at me, threatening to split me open in half.

We were only here for two more nights, leaving on Tuesday to catch our respective flights. But every time I imagined her on that flight back, I was consumed by images of the mischievous eyes that had captivated me. As time was moving closer to our departure, the corny jokes she told to cheer me up scratched the forefront of my mind.

"Actually, I meant to talk to you about that." I could barely keep my voice steady. "I'm not sure if it's a good idea to drive that car back. It was acting up on the way here."

Sooner or later, we'd have to leave; that was inevitable. So, what's the big plan here with this fabrication?

I hadn't a clue.

"Oh." Maya frowned. "Should we take it to a mechanic?"

"Yeah, let's do that."

I made a move toward the bedroom, pretending I'd dress for the day, then stopped as if a realization hit me.

"Fuck, it's a weekend," I empathized with faux remorse. "People in the countryside don't work on Sundays, and we are too remote for Ubers."

"Shit, if that car doesn't work, we are stuck. And my school's starting back up."

Most college kids partied and fooled around. Maya struck me as the kind of person who wasn't late even to the eight a.m. lectures. She anxiously paced at the thought of missing a class for the first time in her life.

I would have laughed if I could ignore the growing ache from her forlorn looks.

I put two fingers to my forehead, rubbing my temple. "Don't worry, baby. I'll take a look at the car. Whatever's wrong, I'm sure I can fix it."

Maya turned on her heels, beaming. She practically jumped into my arms in a childish manner. "My hero!" she quipped.

Her warm embrace mingled with my bitterness. Relief was only emanating through her at the thought of leaving me. I still couldn't think straight. My arms circled her waist, remaining motionless to soak up all the affection she had to offer.

Maya leaned back to speculate, hands on my shoulders. "Thank you, Brandon. I can't miss the first day of classes." But she might if the "malfunctioning" car was still out of order.

Not wanting to resort to tricking her, I had to disprove Maya's apprehensions about us within the small remaining window. And fuck if I didn't try.

For the rest of the day, I conjured up every possible idea the "right man" might have used to woo her—making her breakfast, a nature tour, watching the damn sunset.

Hell, I even took her on a fucking picnic.

I refrained from touching her all day, determined to show her the kind of man I could be. To show her it wasn't only about the physical aspect. Faked as much charm as I could muster without gagging.

Maya appeared contemplative throughout it all, though our conversations never stalled. Except for over one topic.

"How does your family feel about you extending this trip?" I asked, shutting the wooden front door that led into the kitchen.

"Unhappy," Maya answered curtly, dropping her beach bag on the kitchen island.

We felt overheated after the activities in the sun and finally called it quits on our outdoor adventures. Frankly, I was far more concerned with our *indoor* adventures, but it had to wait until this discussion was out of the way.

After our first exchange, I marked 'family' as an unsafe topic, skirting around it. Later, I realized they played an integral role in Maya's hesitation about extending our... acquaintance.

"What did they say?" I pressed, following her into the living room.

Maya stopped in front of the sofa. "It doesn't matter," she dismissed.

"You seem to hate talking about your family."

"So do you," she retorted.

The overgrown branches outside scratched against the glass window. The screeching noise was annoying, yet Maya appeared more peeved about the current discussion.

"Not with you. Ask me anything."

Maya mulled me over for a long minute, opening her mouth several times to phrase a question. Either she lost her nerve or her interest.

"I don't need to. If you want to share, I'm here. But I'm not going to pry," she said at long last.

She meant to add, "*and I hope you don't either*," though she didn't voice it. Instead, she expressed a different thought.

Maya drew closer, hips swaying gently with the motion. "Besides, the last thing I want to do is talk about them when we are together."

The dimness in my vision returned with her proximity. Never had I lost my track of thoughts in the snap of a finger, not like this. She was *that* potent, overwhelming me into a state of intoxication.

Maya took another step closer… and then one more until only a Dewey Decimal of an inch remained between us. I searched her flashing blue eyes implicitly, unable to look away from the sight in front of me.

I was surprised by the complete three-sixty from our conversation. More astonishing was the moment Maya leaned forward to kiss me.

But she didn't just kiss me; she attacked.

Maya threw herself at me with a fierce grunt, mouth crashing against mine, lips full of passion. The force almost toppled me. I was a big guy and stayed in shape. The only reason I stumbled backward was due to the sheer shock value.

For the first time, Maya was kissing me of her own volition.

My patience was already wearing thin from the day. Her boldness broke the last bit of restraint I had exercised. Snaking my hand around her neck, I dragged my lips down the column of her neck for a taste of her skin—heated from the afternoon sun—licking, nipping, and caressing. Creamy, flushed skin blazed like it had been set on fire. I panted hotly in the hollow of her shoulders while Maya's hands moved studiously as if learning every inch of my body.

"Brandon," she moaned in between my biting kisses.

I grabbed fistfuls of hair to yank her head up, our mouths meeting somewhere in the middle due to our height difference.

"I want to..." she whispered against my lips. Her eyes landed on my crotch, hands moving toward the region.

I waited with anticipation. Maya's tranquility from the day was dissipating, displaying her unshackled side. She trailed kisses down my chest, sinking to her knees. Maya peeked up from under a thick set of lashes.

"Show me what to do," she whispered.

Who in the hell was this girl?

Last night, her reluctance knew no bounds, acting like some poster child. Tonight, she was... free.

I didn't understand Maya though one crucial detail became evident. Maya lied about loving her life inside a bubble because I was bearing witness to her natural habitat. She loved being free.

Hair loose, eyes glazed, lusted out face. Underneath the good girl was a heart that could never be tamed, wilder than a mare.

No matter how much she lived by arbitrary rules, Maya had a chaotic side that begged to be free. It couldn't be organized and filed away, not the way she desired. It was only a matter of time before Maya realized it.

My breathing raced at the thought. I whispered instructions, telling her to unzip me, take out my cock and hold it around the base. I never had to tell a woman to deep throat me or stroke me. But there was something so pure about her innocence, yet it was dirty in its own way.

Suppressing a groan, I moved my hand into her silky, golden hair. Precum was already dripping from me, but she was a champ, diving in to let the thick moisture coat her tongue.

I must have growled because Maya's eyes flipped up. Yes, I was definitely growling, "Fuck. Oh… shit," amongst a plethora of other obscenities.

One lick and I was transported to an alternate universe. My heart inflated, beating—no shouting—on its own accord, the sounds escalating to spill out of my mouth.

"Close your mouth over my cock," I hissed.

Maya leaned forward more confidently despite the fear I must have provoked with my unrestrained hunger.

"Holy shit. That's it. Suck me," I rapped out.

She complied without hesitancy, the warmth inside her taking me to paradise. I let her take over to do as she pleased, hands squeezing, mouth moving back and forth. What she lacked in experience, she more than made up for with enthusiasm.

I had never stared at someone in awe like this, never wondered if they enjoyed the moment as much as I did, but that's all I could think of.

"God. Hold still. Look at me."

I held her in my grasp, needing a minute to watch her with her mouth wide open, my dick stretching out her lips. Pouty, pink lips, her heated skin, curtained by straight golden hair… fuck. Letting out a roar, I pulled back and pumped into her.

"Shit!" I came within seconds, cum dripping down her throat.

I stumbled against the side of the couch to find equilibrium and to compose my excited heart. My panting filled the room though Maya remained on her knees, wide eyes watching me inquisitively.

As my vision cleared and my rational senses reinstated, a critical realization dawned on me—Maya was an evil genius.

She gathered that I had become a slave for her tender body after only one night together. More proof that I was acting like a love-sick buffoon. She was using her influence over me to manipulate the situation because Maya wasn't willing to play ball, not about her family.

"Maya," I wheezed, "don't think for a second that our conversation from earlier is over just because you did that."

Maya didn't respond. Instead, she rose, turned on her heels, and adjourned to the bedroom.

My bedroom.

She left the door ajar. Unzipping her blue dress and letting it pool around her ankles, she revealed a blue push-up bra that highlighted her cleavage. Her matching underwear had pencil-thin straps on the sides, allowing an unfiltered view from thigh to breast and that slight curve of her abdomen. She was toned and so goddamn silky smooth all over.

I swallowed.

Without a backward glance, Maya tiptoed to the adjoined bathroom—leaving that door open as well—and filled the tub with steaming water and a concoction of bath products.

Looping her arms back, she unhooked the blue bra, the straps falling away. Firm breasts jutted out, nipples standing to attention and leaving my mouth dry at the sight. As if she hadn't tortured me enough, Maya curved her thumbs under the waistband of her underwear, slowly sliding it down her thighs.

Her eyes flipped back to meet mine, a silent invitation written in them.

A cynical part of me knew better, warning that Maya was doing all of this to distract me. Yet, I followed, mesmerized, letting her win because I didn't have the power to say *no* to her.

The conclusion was drawn even before I stepped into the damn tub and pulled her to my lap, watching her ride my cock as water ran down her lathered breasts. There was nothing more I'd learn about Maya unless she relented, and quite possibly, I didn't know her at all.

Brandon

SHE STOOD with a mug in hand—very much resembling a beggar—before the second pot of coffee had even simmered.

"You look like Oliver Twist. *Please, sir, I want some more,"* I mimicked the desperate way her hands clung to the cup with a thick English accent. Last night, we were up for hours, my appetite for her never weaning. Probably the reason why Maya was inhaling the java this morning. "Do you really need more caffeine in your system?"

Maya smiled sheepishly. "I'm useless without coffee."

"Number one drug in the world," I said, pouring her yet another cup.

She sighed contentedly while my attention diverted to the black yoga pants hugging her thighs and the ribbed tank top—simple but sexy. The outfit made her look younger than the dresses she had sported so far, but it was no less erotic.

I wondered if it'd be unsafe to grope her while she was nursing a piping hot beverage. She was this shiny new toy, and I was the boy who wanted to figure out all of her features and buttons. But surely, I could go five minutes without mauling her.

Turned out that I couldn't. With a tight grip around her waist, I lifted her onto my lap, taking a seat at the kitchen table.

Last night, Maya came out of her shell to play. She matched my hunger until dawn, even when she was sore. Something shifted between us, wiping away all traces of her previous unease.

And I... I was living/breathing every second of it. Maya giggled at my impatient hands on her tits and the lips on her pulse.

"Let's do something memorable today," she suggested.

I nuzzled my nose against her neck. "What did you have in mind?"

"We could go fishing since you never had the chance. I also wanted to check out that cave you mentioned. Oh, and we should definitely have steaks again for dinner."

My stomach tightened. For a moment, I didn't want to realize why she was suggesting these *special* activities, yet it was crystal clear.

"I know it's a pain to work the grill," she rambled on, "but it is our last night together."

I felt as if I couldn't breathe.

Indicating Maya to rise by patting her lower back, I stood to frame. "Last night?" I repeated sharper than intended.

She laughed nervously. "We are supposed to leave first thing tomorrow morning, remember?" Her hand moved up and down my forearm provocatively, suggesting more than just a dinner date. "I want today to be special in every way."

My stomach dropped into an infinite void.

After catering to her this whole damn weekend, this girl was still adamant it would never work outside of these perimeters. For God's sake, I took her on a picnic.

A MOTHERFUCKING PICNIC.

Why in the hell did I put myself through the torture of acting like her goddamn boyfriend?

"Got it. One last fuck to remember me by," I could barely keep the bite out of my tone.

Maya blinked, dropping her hands to her sides. She didn't speak for several minutes.

An excruciating agony chipped away at me from her refusal to deny my accusation. But the grueling thought was outweighed by an irrefutable realization.

I can't let her go or pursue long-distance without guaranteeing a brighter future.

Not only did I want this woman, but the pain I'd experience without her constant presence would be insurmountable. Both of my parents were dead. I wasn't on speaking terms with my stepmother or half-brother. My only living grandparent—grandfather—lived far away.

I preferred this solitary life of mine and an empty home most of the time. But then there were moments when I wondered—if today were my last day on earth, would it really affect anyone?

Would anyone even grieve my death?

Other than the hand-selected childhood friends, I was positive that Maya would be the only person to mourn my loss. Probably cry at my funeral too.

I barely knew her, yet suddenly she was all I had left on this earth. The lone entity to mean something to me. I'd rather we die together in this godforsaken cottage than part ways with her. Deadbolt it, burn it to the ground with both of us still locked inside.

"As much as I'd like to go home, we can't leave tomorrow." My voice was cutting without a trace of the tenderness I had shown her only moments ago.

Maya picked up on it. "What?"

"I checked on the car yesterday; it's the battery." Lies. "It only turns on occasionally, which is fine for a short drive but needs to be replaced before the long-ass one to Nice."

A good lie rested on vague descriptions with some believable details sprinkled on top. Maya had shown no inclination of being car savvy; she didn't even know how to drive one. There was no way to disprove the abstract possibility that a battery glitch during a long drive might leave us stranded.

At the same token, if we needed to leave the premises for groceries, it'd be suspicious if the battery miraculously recovered. Sporadic malfunction was the safest bet.

"Okay," she said tentatively. "The auto shop should be open today, so we can take the car into town."

"And I will." I glanced at her, devoid of emotions. "But it takes days for auto parts to come in. Safer to just reschedule our flights altogether."

"Could we request a rush order for the battery—"

"We are in a remote village, Maya," I sneered, the mocking voice insinuating she was foolish for suggesting it. "Not exactly known for its reliable access to resources."

Maya flinched, though still chock full of dejected hope. "Then let's take the train."

"I can't leave my rental car in Italy," I snapped. Every time she suggested an alternate option, my mind was overwhelmed with this need to hurt her. "I'm liable for returning it to the same location."

Maya tensely twisted her hands, demoralized, lips trembling. "Okay, I guess I can take the train back on my own."

That was the comment to break the camel's back. Her eagerness, begging for a way out, was damn irritating. Downright fucked up. She was so desperate to get away that she'd leave me behind even though we came here together.

I clenched my teeth to grit out, "There are no train stations in a hundred-mile radius."

Maya stilled, watching me with an unreadable expression. It appeared as if a crucial detail had clicked for her.

"Yesterday, we were together all day... and all night." Her voice was low, thick with doubt. "Are you sure you had the time to inspect that car properly?"

Could misleading someone be considered kidnapping?

Technically, I wasn't holding her hostage, simply misinforming her, though I got the distinct impression that Maya didn't believe a single word out of my mouth anymore.

I had been so wary of gaining a reputation as a womanizer in front of my colleagues that I forgot to worry about becoming a kidnapper. In all fairness, I wasn't cognizant of the risk of abduction being added to my LinkedIn profile under skill sets.

"Maya, I run a multimillion-dollar company that I need to get back to... might I add even more so than a college student attending orientation. Do you honestly think I'd propose extending our stay if I weren't absolutely positive it'd be unsafe to drive back?"

Although Maya was on to me, she would have to verify the facts to call my bluff. She didn't poke more holes in my story. Instead, she attempted to dig up sympathy for her cause.

"Brandon, I have a lot to lose if I don't report to the first day of classes." It was barely a whisper, forced agonizingly out of her lips.

I closed my eyes. "Look, at this point, all I can do to help is change your ticket. I should have cell service when I take the car into town if you want to give me the details."

"Rescheduling isn't an option for me," Maya said stubbornly.

"Then there is nothing more I can do for you."

"There is," she argued without missing a beat. "Drive me to a mechanic so we can ask for their professional opinion."

Appalled—that's the face I made at her with my jaw slightly hanging down—a look to indicate pure outrage.

"I get it." My voice was perfectly calm. "You think I made it up to do what... hang around your precious self for a few extra days?" I barked out a hollow laugh that was equal parts cruel. "Don't flatter yourself. I can have any woman on earth without jeopardizing my business or resorting to such antics."

"If that's the case, then why are you trying so hard to keep me here?"

"I'm not trying to keep you here," I hissed. "I'll get the damn car fixed. Until then, I don't want to keep having the same discussion because there is nothing more I can do. You've clearly been sheltered your whole life and don't know how to deal with unexpected predicaments. Sometimes shit happens that's out of our control. It's part of life, so get a goddamn grip on yourself."

The way her expressions flared at my assessment of her life convinced me that I had hit the bull's eye. Maya seemed to exercise excessive restraint to suppress the urge to scream. She hadn't displayed such fury up to this point. It was strangely beautiful.

For an astounding second, I forgot my footing.

"Go to hell, Brandon!" she bellowed. "I'm leaving, even if I have to walk back to Nice. I'm sure I'll find another man who'll be happy to—"

I grabbed her hands and slammed her back against the wall, pinning her wrists to the sides of her head. The raw emotions had elevated, spilling into my senses like lava pouring freely to clog all rational judgment.

She had referred to another man. If she had completed that sentence... The fury had me seeing the world in various shades of red.

"What the hell are you doing?" she screeched, stunned by my actions.

That made two of us.

What the hell was I doing?

She was possibly my last chance at experiencing warmth, the last person to genuinely care for me, and I was ruining it. Maya wriggled to break free, thrashing like a wild animal locked in a cage. Yet, I couldn't let go.

She tried to shove me, but I pushed my body against hers, deliberately crushing her against the wall. It gave me access to her sweet smell and heated skin. My lips floated over her cheekbones while her warmth was... something else entirely.

Our scents intermingled. I dismissed her protests, taking advantage of how I had trapped her. The most sadistic part of me loved it. Loved that she was at my mercy without a way out, my undeniable erection pulsing between us.

With a hand on the nape of her neck, I leaned down, searching for her mouth, but Maya turned away.

For a moment, I did nothing, lazily fingering her hair. My rage was spiking though I kept my expression neutral, letting her make the right decision to turn her face back. We stood there, silently challenging one another, both ferociously wicked in this unidentified cat and mouse game.

Maya retracted first, which seemed uncharacteristic of her. "I shouldn't have said that."

"No, you shouldn't have," I quietly agreed.

I hovered, waiting for Maya to face me.

She refused.

Our time together was progressing at a steady pace until this unfortunate setback. Now, we had confronted each other's inner demons, assessing the other distrustfully, though one thing was for sure—I had this need for her that would never be satiated.

All I wanted to do was throw her on the floor and fuck her brains out until she forgot about her classes or about returning to her stupid life or did anything that didn't involve me.

However, Maya didn't want me right now, and I was resolute not to let this situation deteriorate further.

She is my last hope; I reminded myself over and over.

"I'll take the car into town to see if they can fix it," I whispered gravely against her temple.

I wasn't planning on taking the car to a mechanic, seeing as nothing was wrong with it. I just needed a minute to gather myself before doing something I regretted.

I'd also have cell service in town and could use it to call Aldo. He was employed by my family. Dad was suspicious of anyone trying to take advantage of our money and often employed Aldo's help to run background checks for those we associated with. The resource was handy as I needed to learn about Maya and her mysterious family.

It wasn't like she could leave anyways. This place was too remote and impossible to leave without transportation. The parts about Uber, cell service, and weak Wi-fi were all true.

With her eyes still on another corner of the room, Maya nodded, remaining complacent in my arms. Running my hands through my hair multiple times, I steadied my rampant emotions, but not before dragging her face back for a slow, dominating kiss, hoping to erase our horrific exchange. Things had escalated so quickly between us that we were both left stunned by the turn of events, and I needed to get us back on track.

Maya resisted, giving me nothing in return. Even when I poured my very soul into her with that kiss, Maya remained aloof until I pushed off her.

As I snatched the car keys off the counter, I realized that I came here to say goodbye to my father, yet that goodbye with Maya was the one to almost break me.

Brandon

"BRANDON, THERE IS NO ONE HERE." Milo sighed for the umpteenth time. It made me want to punch the fucker.

"Just give me a second, will you?" I impatiently moved through the rooms. Milo held up his hands in surrender, leaving me be.

I should never have left Maya alone.

After reaching the town center, I called Aldo to run a thorough background check on one Maya Mathews. When I returned later that afternoon, the cottage was deserted, and Maya was long gone.

Frantically, I had searched room after room and the grounds. No traces of her whatsoever. It made no sense. Maya couldn't have left this property without transportation. It was impossible.

My first impulse was to call the police or first responders to search the surrounding areas, but it hadn't been long enough to file a report. A nagging thought had me driving to Nice instead. Her flight was the following day. If she somehow managed to get out of here, that'd be the destination.

Aldo called during my anxious drive.

"What do you have for me?" I had simultaneously picked up the phone along with my speed on the deserted road.

"I wanted to double-check the spelling for the name you gave me."

"Why?" I snapped, urgency spiking with every passing minute.

"Because I can't find a Maya Mathews that fits your description. Are you sure she lives in Paris?"

"Positive." I had memorized every detail on Maya's ID when I first glanced at it.

"I tried multiple variations of the name and the ID number. It's a fake."

"What!" I slammed the brakes abruptly. If there were cars behind me, it would have led to a pile-up.

Aldo explained that every detail I had given him was off by a number or two, making the ID seemingly real to the naked eye without amounting to much. The peculiarity of the situation only intensified upon my arrival at the hotel I had stayed the night I met Maya.

"What do you mean you don't remember her?" I hissed at the bartender. "You asked for her ID right in front of me."

So far, my search had been futile. There wasn't a trace of Maya at the cottage. Aldo couldn't locate any person by the name of Maya Mathews. The bartender didn't remember her, so I went to the hotel manager, demanding the surveillance footage from the night in question. Several "this is unorthodox" and rejections later, they relented, only to find out that the footage had been wiped out, leaving me to harass the poor bartender once again.

The second round of interrogation ticked him off. "Sir, as I already explained, there were many guests at the bar on Friday night. I don't remember everyone."

"Brandon!"

I closed my eyes at Tasha's irritatingly loud voice (or was her name Farah?). I wasn't expecting to run into her, but a eureka flashed in my mind.

Tasha/Farah was also present that night.

"I didn't know you were still in Nice." She moved closer to me.

"Hey! Do you recall the girl I was with on Friday night?" I had cut right to the chase, dismissing all formalities.

Tasha/Farah appeared contemplative, tapping her lips with her thumb. "Umm..."

"Blonde. Thin. Blue eyes." I attempted to jog her memory. "I left with her at the end of the night."

She simply squinted her eyes, perplexed.

I suppressed the urge to yell at her. "We were standing here, remember?"

"Yes, I remember that part."

"Then you turned to look at the girl I was with. She was sitting right there." I pointed at a bar stool. "I was talking to her all night long."

Tasha/Farah frowned. "Brandon, I don't remember you talking to anyone that evening."

Her declaration ended the limited restraint I had exercised throughout that Twilight Zone of a day. The profanities I threw at Tasha/Farah... let's just say my mother wouldn't have been proud.

"You are such a fucking bitch and an ugly one at that. You saw her with your own damn eyes, but you're lying to get back at me because I wouldn't fuck you."

This continued for several minutes until Tasha/Farah was in tears, and the security guards escorted me out for harassing the hotel staff and patrons alike. Unfortunately, I didn't go down without a fight, landing my ass in jail.

Without any alternate options, I grudgingly called Milo to bail me out. He was in Greece for business. Luckily, Nice was only a short hop and a flight away.

Milo didn't pose a single question about my state, judgmental eyes reflecting that finding me in jail one day was all too predictable.

Didn't care.

The unnerving truth was boggling every cell of my being. Maya had turned my life upside down, only to vanish into thin air. Refusing to accept that truth, I forced Milo to drive us back to the place that started my demise—the stupid cottage.

It was in pristine condition, which meant that the groundskeeper had visited. All the sofa cushions were perfectly fluffed out. Dishes in the sink were put away. Beds were tidy. No trash in the house. Even the bathtub had been bleached. As if no one had visited in months.

The house appeared abandoned, further making me look like a mad man.

"Look, dude," Milo started after I exhausted my search for any miscellaneous items left behind by Maya. "I know you have been going through a lot. Sometimes grief can make people see things that aren't there—"

"I'm not fucking crazy," I shouted.

Numerous sources had already echoed the sentiment—Aldo, the hotel staff, the police. Before releasing me, they recommended a psych evaluation, suggesting that I made Maya up to cope with the loss of my dad.

To be honest, there were indications throughout the weekend to suggest Maya was a figment of my imagination. She was too good to be true, checking off the boxes I desired in a woman. And she often verbalized words exactly how I wanted to hear them.

She even resembled a favorite of mine from the past—Mia.

Mia was the only kid I could connect and relate to. The only one who had the brains to challenge me and kept my mind occupied for hours with her eclectic observations. The only person I had drawn a correlation between my sad childhood and hers.

Who better to commiserate with after losing my father than Mia? If someone understood a complicated relationship with their father, it was her. Or, in her case, it was a complicated relationship with Milo—her father figure.

Was it in the realm of possibility that I took the best of Mia's qualities and turned her into an imaginary character able to console me during this time of need? Was all of this my twisted way of dealing with Dad's death?

I quickly dismissed the notion.

No, Maya was real.

Correction. *Maya is real.*

She was more real than anything else on earth. I could still feel her... her touch... the warmth.

"I'm not saying you're crazy," Milo placated. "I'm saying that last weekend was a lot to process."

"Doesn't mean I made up an imaginary woman to bring back to this cottage."

"Brandon, think rationally for a second. In the past, you described this house as your favorite place in the world. Why would you bring a woman here after meeting her once at a bar?"

How the fuck was I to explain what happened to me? Everything with Maya was so out of character for me that it only fueled the story's implausibility.

"I-I just did," was all I could mutter.

"That's what's confusing. You never even look at a girl twice. And now you want me to believe... what... that you are in love with this woman or something?"

I didn't deny the accusation.

Milo, who was generally reserved with his expressions, looked so taken back by my silence that I knew I had lost the last speck of credibility. He didn't believe me for shit.

For the first time since he picked me up from the police station, Milo voiced no more opinions, nor did he lecture me.

I closed my eyes. "Listen, man. I-I just need you to trust me. It was a coincidence that no one else saw her, but she was real. It happened," I emphasized, embedding the thought deep inside me.

Leaning against the wall, Milo crossed his arms across his chest. His face was covered in either sadness or pity; I wasn't entirely sure which one. Neither of us spoke again, quietly listening to the never-ending branches scratching at the windowpane.

* * *

Six Months Later

To say things were rough was putting it mildly. Losing my parents paled in comparison with losing Maya. It made no fucking sense to mourn someone I barely knew. Not to mention, others had declared the entire episode as temporary insanity.

I tried to move on, tried to leave it all behind. Returned to New York and everything. But the very first step into my home ruled out the possibility of resuming my old life.

An immaculately beautiful condo greeted me, yet I couldn't force myself to step inside. It was deafeningly quiet, dull, empty—lacking in all happiness. I stood at the front door, waiting for things to change.

It didn't.

This house needed to be loud, filled with a particular woman's giggles, spouting on endlessly with her talkative nature.

Still, it remained lifeless.

My legs moved on their own—unable to take the silence—exiting the apartment building and into a taxi, finding myself back at the airport.

Fuck returning to that hollow life.

Fuck everyone else.

No one else understood the kind of loss I was experiencing and how meaningless my life had suddenly become. She lived in Paris. If there was a chance, a smidgen of the possibility of finding her, then I had to search the city, live there if need be, comb through every alley.

And that's precisely what I did... for several months. New York for work, then off to Paris at every chance, searching for a nameless girl.

I had to stop.

Many times, I tried to eradicate all thoughts of her. I failed miserably, the void inside me only growing with each passing day.

And then there was the maddening lust.

My body craved her touch, desperate to feel her pulse around my cock again, to watch her perky tits bounce as I fucked her... Goddamnit.

This desire for her was so sickening in its need that it left me with the urge to empty my guts out. The erotic thoughts of her had my hands trembling, my body ready to burst, screaming that I couldn't take one more second without feeling her writhe underneath me.

Like a hole punctured in a plastic water bottle, life was seeping out of me until one day, I knew it'd end with meeting my maker.

This—how I was living my life—wasn't feasible. Something had to change, but nothing could fill the emptiness she had left me with.

At this point, I was fairly certain that I had cooked up the entire weekend because Maya was what I needed to get through my father's death. Even as a fictional character from my imagination, she had instilled such faith in me that I was ready to spend an eternity in search of that feeling once more. Optimism was funny like that, never allowing you to diminish the light flickering within.

In my determined attempt to cling onto hope, I found myself in Nice once again for the damn bi-annual convention.

Only six months ago, I had met Maya right here. Same hotel, same convention, same bar, but luckily, new management who didn't recognize my face. I even sat in the same damn chair to set up the exact scenario.

I didn't expect the night to amount to anything. Yet, I already knew—I'd return until the end of my days in hopes that she'd show up one day.

Part two

Mia

I PRESSED my index and middle fingers on my wrists, counting the beats every fifteen seconds. My heartbeat had dropped from the last tally, and my extremities went numb minutes ago.

The cold was spreading, but it was crucial not to panic at the threat of hypothermia. Any form of exertion would deplete the limited oxygen. It's something I read about.

"Repose," I said to myself.

I read a lot, especially about Mom's on and off depression. As of late, she barely moved from her post. Prolonged bed rest led to inflammation and body aches, something else I read about in the DSM manual.

In an attempt to Feng Shui my mother out of her room to a different locale, this morning I had proposed to stay home and binge on some good old television in the living room. I also had an ulterior motif—Brandon Cooper was supposed to appear on some boring daytime television show. It was meant to be good exposure for his company, and I was excited to see Brandon shine during his big moment.

However, Raven and Reid had put a stop to my pleas to skip one lousy day of eighth grade. I was twelve and the baby of the family. It was customary that the ideas of the youngest member be ignored by default.

I wasn't ready to give up so easily. When their faces disappeared from my line of vision on the way to school, I turned around and returned home. The only person aware that I had skipped school today was Mom. She was excited to have the company and said it could be our little secret.

The decision could only be defined as my most recently discovered SAT word—dismal.

I was dying to watch Brandon's TV segment but was distracted by Mom's face that kept twisting in pain from the prolonged bed rest. Ice packs generally soothed bed sores. So, I went to our basement searching for one and was rummaging through the top shelf of our walk-in freezer when the door slammed shut, locking me in. The hinges had been malfunctioning, the reason why Milo didn't want anyone going into the freezer.

The fifteen-by-fifteen walk-in freezer had two shelves on each side. It contained boxes of food Milo had purchased in bulk. The cold ground, the door, and the remaining wall were all made from steel, and there was no light unless someone opened the door.

Pitch black.

No way out, nor was anyone looking for me. I even left my cell phone upstairs.

Normally, I would throw a massive fit and scream my head off. However, no one would hear me from upstairs, and it was paramount to keep up the well-paced breathing.

"Paramount," I translated another SAT word from my mind to lips. It was the first time my word choices weren't a hindrance.

I was surrounded by older family members and introduced to mature topics early, along with advanced literature. I had the tendency to copy the adults in my life, relying heavily on the power of observation to speak the way everyone else around me did. My word choices often propelled responses such as, *"Mia, stop talking like a grown-up."*

Meanwhile, my vocabulary failed to be a driving force in building camaraderie at school. And my tendency to articulate acute observations was deemed cruelly honest at times, leading to limited interactions with kids my age.

Though my friends or family didn't appreciate my candor or word choices during our exchanges, my large vocabulary finally served a purpose. If I could remember the SAT words from this year's list, then my mind was still sharp, meaning that the cold hadn't set in yet. Confusion was the first symptom of hypothermia, followed closely by slurred speech.

"Obfuscate."

A magazine article about surviving in Antarctica had detailed hypothermia prevention tips, especially in situations where oxygen was scarce. Never thought an article about Antarctica could apply to New York City life.

With my back against the floor, I built a fort with food boxes to shield myself from the cold. It wasn't working. My hope now rested on my brothers since Mom probably wouldn't realize that I was missing.

"Abandon," I murmured, slightly dozing off.

Must not pass out.

I tried to verbalize the next SAT word but couldn't remember it. Crap!

Shutting my eyes tight, I prayed to God to somehow signal my brother. Milo was always my one shining hope. No matter what, I had to keep faith that God would pass this message onto him.

"Mia!"

Was that a hallucination or an answer to my prayers?

Faintly, barely, I heard footsteps shuffling. It had been hours, so Reid and Raven must be back from school. Milo was also due home from college. His classes today ended in the afternoon. That spark of hope reignited. I dragged my palm to flap it against the freezer door.

"Inn hre!"

The panic-stricken footsteps drew closer. "Mia!"

There were now multiple voices in my proximity. With the last bit of remaining energy, I slammed my hand against the freezer door once more.

"I heard a noise coming from the freezer."

"Fuck!"

The door flew open. Milo's distinct scent surrounded me as I was picked up from the floor.

"I knw you'd comeee," I slurred incoherently. "Never gave uuuup. Knew... you save me."

* * *

Reid and Raven returned home from school to find a voicemail from my principal. They panicked to hear about my absence and called Milo, who went into high alert upon finding out that I had left my phone behind. I'd never make that mistake, so Milo checked every crevice of our mansion of a home.

My brothers found me huddled on the floor of the freezer, covered in boxes and attempting to blabber big words into the air. When I tried to explain the logic behind it, they decided that the hypothermia had set in.

My family members didn't welcome my quirky nature with open arms.

At least, I convinced them against taking me to the Emergency Room, though it took a lot of persuading. Hospital visits had occurred far too many times in the past, and I was positive that a social worker out there was racking up a file on me.

Milo and Reid brought me back to my room instead. Raven was quick to change me out of my clothes, stacking blankets on me no matter how many times I repeated, "I'm fine."

While Raven fussed over me, Milo sat at my desk with his laptop open.

Odd.

The oldest of our lot and eight years my senior, Milo never missed an opportunity to lecture us. Whenever something bad happened, Milo spent hours giving us tips to avoid such disasters in the future.

Whereas today, he had only demonstrated serenity since the incident. As usual, he was dressed casually in jeans and a white t-shirt. However, I never let the nonchalant appearance fool me. It was the calm before the storm.

Milo still hadn't looked up from his emails when Reid strolled into the room with a second tray of hot drinks. Reid's resemblance to Milo was eerie with his six-foot frame, deep voice, and broad build. Despite their four-year age gap, the only stark physical difference between them was the eyes—Reid's were glacial blue while Milo's were emerald green.

Not to be outshined by the boys, Raven rivaled Milo and Reid in the looks department and was dubbed snow white for her jet-black hair, fair complexion, and rosy features.

All three looked like they were part of some exotic poster-perfect ad. In comparison, I was blonde and skinny. There was nothing exceptional about my appearance, and, more than once, others found it hard to believe that I belonged to the same family.

"Are we hypothermia-free yet?" Reid asked briskly.

"Yes!" I huffed, fed up with being a patient. The covers were counterproductive—overheating my body.

Raven shook her head at Reid to overturn my *yes.* Why had I bothered to respond? No one actually spoke *to* me; they spoke *around* me.

At sixteen, Reid and Raven also exercised some parental authority over me. They were both juniors in high school and childhood best friends despite Reid being a sulky teenager—always angry at Mom or Milo—while Raven was even-keeled.

Still, Raven and Reid's cosmic connection was awe-inspiring. They were born on the same day, one hour apart, to fathers who also happened to be childhood best friends, practically brothers. Our two families were so close that we referred to Raven's dad as our uncle. And when Raven's parents had to leave the country due to some unforeseen events, Dad volunteered to take Raven in so she could finish school in America.

It was ironic because soon after, Dad also got the opportunity of a lifetime as a visiting physician in Grand Cayman. He now traveled back and forth between New York and the Cayman Islands. The times he was gone, Mom was in charge, which really meant that Milo was in charge since Mom's mood was eternally fluctuating.

With Dad's absence, Raven's diplomatic personality brought a lot to the table. And over the years, she had become my pseudo sister.

"Do you know that hypothermia is just another word for overheating? You guys might be doing more damage than good at this point," I informed.

Reid quirked an eyebrow. "What did we tell you about being a know-it-all?"

I stuck my tongue out, which had scalded due to the sheer volume of hot beverages Raven insisted that I consume. "That I should do it more often?" I suggested.

Mom made her presence known from the door frame, interrupting our lively debate. "Hi, sweetheart. How are you feeling now?"

Three heads snapped in the direction of the door, eyes filled with hostility. Meanwhile, I tried to slink away under the comforter, silently communicating with Mom to make a run for it. This wasn't a safe zone. My siblings were out for blood—Mom being their prime target.

"What are you doing?" Reid gritted out. "We told you not to come in here."

The guilt hung heavily on Mom. She had been lurking in the hallway all afternoon to see me. However, Milo and Reid made it clear she was unwelcome.

Truth be told, all I wanted was my *mommy* after today's ordeal, but I didn't have the balls to challenge my brothers. They harbored a deep-seated resentment toward Tessa Sinclair. It was difficult to justify choosing her over them—or anyone else for that matter—especially after they rescued me yet again. I knew my brothers would save me when I was stuck in that freezer. I didn't have the same expectation out of Mom.

Unlike my brothers, I understood that Mom suffered from a scatterbrain personality due to her issues. I was forgiving. They were cynical.

"I-I just wanted to see how Mia was doing." Mom nervously twisted her hands together.

"Oh! So, now you care?" Reid sneered, making me flinch.

"Reid," Raven gently reprimanded to simmer the friction.

"No, Rave," he snapped. "Don't defend her. Not over this."

Everyone was angry at Mom for letting me play hooky, then failing to realize I was missing for hours. She fell asleep on the couch, only to be woken up by Raven and Reid's arrival from school. It was an honest mishap.

I got stuck in a walk-in freezer because of my dumb decision, not Mom's. I never skipped school before, and the universe taught me a valuable lesson on my first try. I didn't want Mom to pay the price for my mistake.

No matter what Reid or Milo said, I knew Mom would get better one day, but not if everyone was always ganging up on her.

Mom needed the support of her family, and a fallout might throw her into the deep end.

"I'm sorry," Mom uttered faintly, breaking my heart. "I fell asleep. I didn't realize—"

"Are you even listening to yourself? How many times did Mia end up in the hospital because you weren't paying attention to your own damn child? It's a shock that social services haven't taken her away from us already."

"Reid, calm down," Milo drawled, standing to his full height to command the attention of the room.

Milo played every bit of the older brother role—calm, collected, responsible, and... hella intimidating. What he established with short resolute words, most people couldn't transmit with tenacious explanations.

While he was warm, Milo kept us at arm's length. With Dad's odd work hours and Mom's issues, Milo learned early on that he needed to detach from us to do what was necessary. He wasn't groomed for the role, but leadership came easy. Milo was the golden boy, on track to graduate Columbia with honors and a growing business on the side. He also knew half the tri-state area. Everyone loved and respected him.

Unfortunately, Reid was the only person who constantly challenged Milo's authority. "I'm not going to calm down. There have to be consequences for what happened today. For God's sake, she almost got Mia killed," Reid shouted the last part. "Just a few more hours and..."

The room turned deafeningly quiet as they absorbed Reid's unspoken premonition. I turned to Raven, begging with my eyes to defend Mom before they tore her into pieces. While no one in this house listened to me, they heeded Raven's opinions. She was the voice of reason.

Not a single word from Raven.

The tension in the room spiked between the four of them. Mom appeared flabbergasted by it all. With her eyes downcast, she stared at a spot on the floor.

Milo stepped forward. "There *will* be consequences."

He didn't have to categorize the consequences to scare Mom. She cracked. "I-I didn't do anything," she whispered, lips trembling.

"Exactly. Your daughter went missing for hours, and you didn't do a thing." Milo shook his head, disappointed. "Mom, I'm doing my best to raise these kids... *your* kids, might I add. At this point, it's whatever that you don't take care of them. At least, don't make my job more difficult. You should have texted me if you knew Mia skipped school, mainly because she has never done it before and only stayed home to make *you* feel better."

"That's not why I stayed home," I exclaimed before snapping my mouth shut. There was an unwritten rule not to contradict Milo in front of others. I rarely spoke up against him, but I couldn't let everyone villainize Mom.

"You are right." Mom closed her eyes, somewhere between humiliated and ashamed. "I... I'll do better from now on. I-I'll wake up in the mornings and... make breakfast before everyone goes to school. Pack the lunches too."

Milo snorted as if he couldn't believe the words she uttered. "No, Mom. I can't have you near them anymore, not unless Dad is here to supervise you," Milo spoke without an ounce of emotion in his voice. "This is becoming dangerous. I already spoke to Dad, and he agrees."

My back straightened, neck prickling with awareness. I didn't fear Milo's stern voice. It was the cold, rational one that made me squirm.

"What do you mean?"

Milo stared at Mom coolly. "You're going to stay with Dad until the end of his assignment. I booked you a flight to Grand Cayman. You are leaving... tonight."

"Whoa," Reid intervened. Even Raven's head snapped up, taken aback.

"No!" I cried out.

Milo couldn't do this. He wouldn't. Raven and Reid were best friends. They had each other and a huge group of friends. Whereas all the kids my age thought I was weird. I had Milo, but he had too much on his plate, along with a vast social circle. With his attention divided amongst the three of us, there was only so much one person could do.

Mom was all I had.

"Milo, I'm sorry. I swear, I didn't stay home to make Mom feel better. I wanted to—"

"Milo," Reid interjected as if I hadn't spoken. "I'm angry at Mom too, but this is extreme."

"I'm not angry. This decision is purely logical."

"But it wasn't her fault," I tried to chime in.

"This is ridiculous," Mom said shrilly, voice rising with panic. "I'm not leaving my own house. I'm the parent here. You don't get to make those kinds of decisions, Milo."

A speck of hope flickered at Mom's rebuttal. Though Milo's word was generally the law in our household, I reminded myself that Mom was the parent. Milo couldn't throw her out.

"Maybe we all need to take a deep breath and a step back," Raven spoke calmly. "Let's just think rationally before jumping into rash decisions."

"There is nothing to think about. My mind is made up."

"Please, Milo," I wailed. "I'm sorry. I'm sorry. I won't do it again; I'll never skip school. Please don't send her away."

They ignored me, busy bickering amongst themselves.

"Come on, Milo," Raven sounded sympathetic toward Mom's plight. "Tearing this family apart isn't the answer. We... we'll just have to keep better tabs on each other from now on."

"Exactly," Reid agreed. "This won't solve anything."

"You can't kick me out of my own house!" Mom screeched. "I'm not leaving. I'm not. I'm staying here with my children."

"She didn't even do anything," I choked. "It was *my* fault. I stayed home because I wanted to see Brandon on TV."

Yet again, no one heard me. Sitting in a room surrounded by my siblings, I had never felt more alone.

"Mom, this isn't the first, second, or even the third time something like this has happened," Milo only addressed Mom, ignoring everyone else. "I can't take care of these kids if I'm constantly picking up after you."

Milo closed the gap between them and spoke in a low voice that was difficult to make out.

"I love you, Mom," he whispered. "But I need you out of this house. You know, as well as I do, that it isn't good for them to be around you. They are watching you... your behavior... and it's impacting them."

The lack of fight remaining in Mom's eyes activated my dreaded emotions. Or quite possibly, it was because everyone refused to hear my side of the story. Or perhaps I was angry at myself for skipping school to see Brandon on TV. But the most likely reason was triggered by the fear of loneliness.

Mom was the only person constantly available, no matter the time of day. Even if she weren't lucid, at least she was *here*. This was truly a ghost house without her, and I couldn't fathom the loneliness.

I started screaming hysterically, throwing limbs and objects alike. Everything in the vicinity suffered my wrath. The cups on the tray sitting on my nightstand met their end against the wall, crashing and burning. The pillows and heaps of blankets landed on the floor. I said awful, horrible things, things I could never take back.

Reid cursed out loud. Raven tried to shush me. Mom shielded herself with two hands in front of her face while Milo grabbed something off my desk.

I couldn't see clearly; my vision was blurred, ears thudding, though I heard every instruction Milo vocalized.

"Raven, we have to leave for the airport in a couple of hours. Take Mom to her room and help her pack whatever fits in two check-in bags. I'll send the rest of her stuff later."

"No. Not a single argument, Mom. You have done enough."

"Reid, find a broom. Grab some paper towels, too. And lose the damn attitude."

I was hiccupping and wheezing from the lack of breathing. Milo never acknowledged my tantrums. Never tried to calm me down like Raven did. We had a drill of our own.

An inhaler was shoved in my mouth while a heavy book landed on the bed next to me. Milo patiently pressed down the top of the inhaler and waited for my breathing to normalize.

Minutes passed. My hiccupping subsided, and my hair was matted down. Out of nowhere, Milo grabbed the heavy book off the bed.

"I read a chapter in this book that I think might be relevant to something I'm going through. I have this professor I can't stand. And after every one of his classes, I end up hitting the gym because it's better to take it out on a punching bag than him."

Predictable. Milo was baiting me with a posed hypothetical problem.

He tapped the hardcover of the book thoughtfully with an index finger. "I realized that I was exhibiting one of the behaviors listed here, but I can't remember what it was. It's been driving me crazy all day."

"Good," I chewed out resentfully.

"I think it was a type of defense mechanism," he said casually.

I didn't contribute to the conversation, feeling stubborn.

"But which one?" Milo opened the book, pensive eyes skimming the pages. "Which one? Which one? Damnit... it's at the tip of my tongue."

Oh, for God's sake.

"Displacement," I declared, then immediately scolded myself for taking the bait so easily. Walked right into that one, didn't I?

"No, you're wrong."

I fisted my hands at my side. "No, I'm not," I ground out, irritated. "Redirecting anger from the original source to something else. That's classic Displacement."

Any mild satisfaction from my explanation was tempered by Milo's unconvinced expression. He frowned, dismissing my theory. "Actually, it's Sublimation, not Displacement," he corrected mildly.

"What?" I huffed.

"It'd be Displacement if I had channeled my anger toward a loved one, which is frowned upon. Sublimation is a mature version of a defense mechanism—redirecting your emotions toward a socially acceptable target, such as a punching bag."

"Give me that." I snatched the book from his hand.

My eyes widened as I opened the chapter about defense mechanisms. The theories were virtually similar, but Milo was smart enough to phrase it in such a way that I overlooked it rather than differentiating between the two.

The complexity of his question caught my attention... and my respect. Feeling humbled, I read through all the examples of each defense mechanism.

Before long, Milo phrased another sophisticated question of similar stature, and I scrambled to answer. He charged ahead, quizzing me about more material. My responses were correct until another trick question bested me.

It was rare when I didn't know an answer, forcing my inquisitiveness. I asked for a hint. Milo didn't give me one, so I returned to the book. It would seem that my grasp on the content wasn't strong.

Eventually, Milo left me to dig out the solution by myself.

The world was lost to me by the time Mom came by to bid me farewell. Comprehension settled in that Milo was simply distracting me from the temper tantrum and our home situation. By that point, I was physically exhausted from the day's exertions and mentally drained from the difficult material Milo had challenged me with.

I could do no more than hug my mother goodbye before sinking into a dark hole.

Chapter 11

Mia

"Pouting gives you permanent frown lines," Brandon declared. His attempts at consolation were terrible.

"That's not true." I pouted more, still trapped under a mound of blankets—Milo's orders. "And I don't care if I get frown lines."

"Sure, you do," he countered.

Usually, I loved bantering with Brandon, but I was annoyed at life tonight. "Why would I care about that?"

"Same reason you watch all those YouTube videos to learn about skincare and makeup. You like beauty."

Surprised, I tilted my face toward him. Brandon sat five feet away on the recliner chair. With his signature smirk in place, he appeared arrogant about figuring me out.

Most of the time, I was beyond flattered if Brandon took an interest in my life or knew something specific about me. But tonight, he was the last person I wanted to see. Earlier today, I skipped school to see him on live TV. I paid dearly for my little rebellion and was determined never to break Milo's rules again.

I turned away, pressing my face against the pillow. "You don't have to entertain me," I informed sulkily.

Brandon picked up on my grouchy mood and matched it with his own. "I'm not entertaining you," he snapped. "I'm here because your brother will have my head if I leave."

Unlike others, Brandon never gave me a pass because of my age. That's what I loved the most about him.

"I'm also here because you are usually tolerable for a kid. So, stop acting like a brat."

I clenched my jaw at his choice of word, throat bobbing with more unshed tears. I was still facing the wall when I heard Brandon's relented sigh, followed by shuffling. The mattress dipped as he sat next to me on the bed.

"Mia, it sucks that you had such a rough day." This time he spoke in a gentler tone. "But today was harder on Milo."

I tensed.

"Milo was the one who had to make that difficult decision," Brandon added. "And he did it because he loves you more than his own mother."

Presumably, it was challenging for Brandon to paint Milo as the savior. However, the brutal honesty resonated with me. Milo didn't wear his heart on his sleeve, so I had no idea whether the decision was difficult to make.

"You aren't like other kids, Mia," Brandon pressed. "You know better than to act this way."

I closed my eyes again. Why was Brandon the only person to see through my shit?

I wanted to be grown like everyone else. While I understood hidden connotations, picked up on adult lingo, and retained an extensive vocabulary from my reading list (all in my attempt to belong in that exclusive grown-up clique), the jury was out on the most crucial component of all—my age.

A part of me wanted to scream and yell and throw a fit. I

couldn't control it. This could be a classic case of teenage hormones, though I was still a few months shy of thirteen. This sort of behavior could also stem from boredom. I wondered if Milo suspected the same since he constantly distracted me, loading me with so much extra material outside of classes that it made the curriculum at school appear uninspired.

Unfortunately, the ugliest side of me still showed itself today. Afterward, my siblings left to drop Mom off at the airport. Worried I might throw another tantrum, Milo preemptively subdued me by assigning Brandon the role of my glorified babysitter. Growing up, I had a crush on Brandon. Milo didn't find it amusing when I used to run around betrothing myself to him, but he had hoped for Brandon's presence to appease me tonight.

Unfortunately, it had the opposite effect.

It was humiliating that Brandon had to see me in this capacity. I was this ugly kid with a mouth full of braces, snotty nose, and tangled hair. And he was this beautiful man—so damn tall with dark hair and pale blue eyes.

The physical aside, Brandon wasn't all perfect. He was slightly self-centered, regularly forgetting crucial facts and details. He never paid attention to others unless they mattered to *him*. Twice, he forgot my age and grade in school, which saddened me because I wasn't important enough for him to remember.

On the flip side, there was more to Brandon than being an egotistical asshole. If you dug deeper, there were good qualities that I regularly witnessed. Brandon was nice to me, especially in moments when I needed kindness. And he gave me shit when I deserved it, making me realize that the current mannerisms weren't a good look on me.

I wiped my tears away. "I'm embarrassed about the way I acted today," I mumbled, voice still cracked from my earlier screaming fit.

"Hmm." I could hear Brandon's smug smile, my heart doing a flip at the sound it made. "That's a start."

"Can we please just drop it?" I slanted my head in his direction, changing the subject. "Do you know any good stories?"

Brandon chuckled. "No, little Bunny. I don't."

When I was little, Milo affectionately called me Rabbit because of my overbite. I got braces a year ago. Brandon was the only one to suggest against it. He said my overbite gave me character, and in fact, my adorable overbite deserved an even cuter name. Brandon dubbed me Bunny because it was more endearing than Rabbit. Even before he christened me with that name, I knew he was my first crush—a fact that's true to the day.

"Aren't you a little too old for bedtime stories?" he cocked an eyebrow.

"That's not why I asked. I have to write a short story for a competition Milo signed me up for. I need inspiration."

"This is the hundredth competition your brother has signed you up for." Brandon rose from the bed and strolled to my desk. "Your desk is a fucking mess."

Despite my age, Brandon never spoke with a filter around me. That included cursing, lots of it. At least, he didn't reprimand me for speaking like an adult or lied to me whenever I asked him grown-up questions.

"What are you looking for?" I stared quizzically at his back.

"Fuck. Is this a candy wrapper? Can't even find a pen in this disaster zone. Is disorganization the price you paid to become a genius?"

I rolled my eyes. Brandon called me a mad scientist. He was immaculate, whereas I was haphazard, but I was in no mood to clean up. "If you don't stop giving me shit, I'll tell my brother that I learned all my curse words from you."

"No one likes a tattletale," he chided inattentively though I knew Brandon didn't care. In fact, he loved to antagonize and would probably enjoy going head-to-head with Milo.

Brandon returned, a rollerball pen and a bunch of vintage-style script paper in hand. "These are the only blank pieces of paper I could find."

"It was for an art project to make a Victorian-styled book."

"Do you still need them?"

"No. But what are we using them for?"

"To write your story," he replied easily.

"Now?" I sat up, legs crossed.

"No time like the present." Brandon shuffled the blank parchment papers and handed me the pen.

"I guess," I said tentatively, tucking free strands of hair behind my ear.

"How do you want to start?"

I shrugged. "We need a storyline... and a name for the protagonist."

"Maya," Brandon suggested without a second thought.

Jealousy sank into me at his hasty response. "Came up with that pretty quickly. New girlfriend?" I half-heartedly laughed, though my insides were frozen.

Brandon playfully punched me under the jaw. "Maya sounds just like Mia. It'll be easy to write a character and story based on yourself."

Feeling bold, I blurted out, "Then we should also write a character just like you." I thought for a second. "Bran. Brany. No, wait. Bran-Bran."

A playful smile tugged at his lips. Brandon didn't protest the emasculating name, much too comfortable in his own skin. "Mathews," he declared instead.

"Excuse me?"

"Her full name—Maya Mathews."

I blinked at his determined face to get on with it. With a heavy sigh, I put pen to paper, unconvinced this "Maya Mathews" was made up, considering how quickly he procured it. I was shocked when Brandon, of all people, proposed that we write a love story.

"Will there be any sex scenes in this love story?"

"No." He didn't flinch but added as an afterthought, "Aren't you a little young to know about sex scenes?"

"Raven already gave me the bird and the bees convo. She said kids in New York City were too fast, and I needed to learn this information from reliable sources rather than be misinformed."

"Little too young for that talk if you ask me," he mumbled.

"But I have known about sex for years. It's the union of genitalia accompanied by rhythmic movements."

"What do you mean you have known for years?" Brandon lurched back in shock.

"I read about sex in books. What's the big deal?" I asked, genuinely confused by his reaction. Coitus was a natural part of life. The male reproductive organ had to enter the female channel so our species wouldn't die out. "I thought sex was supposed to be pleasurable other than just for copulation."

Brandon shuddered.

"I'm pretty sure there are a few sexually active girls in my class," I added.

Brandon's eyes almost bugged out of their sockets. "Kids in your class? That's way too young."

"Is that so? How old were you during your first time?" At twelve, I was the youngest in my class, but most of the girls in my grade were fourteen. I knew for a fact that Milo and Brandon were around that age when they first started.

Brandon hesitated. This was a first. He had never been uncomfortable answering my questions before.

I rolled my eyes at the hypocrisy. "I already overheard Alexa that Milo was only thirteen during his first time. You couldn't have been too far behind."

"Don't you have anything better to do than eavesdrop on other people's conversations?"

"I didn't eavesdrop; I overheard," I corrected. "It isn't my fault people forget I'm there and keep talking about inappropriate things."

Brandon paused. "What do you mean people forget you are there?" It was unusual for him to change the topic during one of our debates.

I lifted my right shoulder. "Whenever I'm around, others eventually forget that I'm still in the room."

For several seconds, Brandon didn't speak. "I never forget when you are there," he said at last.

"I know."

I had the urge to erase the sudden pity flashing in his eyes. Brandon's irritation, sarcasm, and entitled attitude didn't bother me. But this... this look of pity... it bothered me a whole lot.

I refused to be his charity case.

"It's no big deal. Should we get back to the story?" I suggested, hoping he'd end with these forlorn looks.

Brandon nodded, eyes flickering to the paper. We didn't let the previous conversation fester as words flew onto the pages, mainly because he spoke faster than I could write. I provided suggestions, too, tweaking the story as necessary.

While on vacation, two broken souls meet and fall in love, only to realize they are better off without one another. Disheartened, they part ways, a piece of them survived by the other.

We named our story, *A Chance Encounter.* It was a complex love story far beyond my time, yet innocent enough to be age-appropriate.

This story would definitely win the competition.

Furthermore, the plot was made for us. The male character was like Brandon—snarky, grumpy, slightly arrogant, yet sweet at the right moments. And Maya might as well be a carbon copy of Mia, except she was an improved version. She was quirky with a solid moral compass and a short fuse. She was also beautiful, talented, and everything else I sought to be.

I listened intently as Brandon shared more of himself than ever before to create a character who thought just like him. But as Brandon went on about this Maya character, that's when my intent staring competed with my hearing.

Brandon described traits that I could only assume as his desired ones in a partner. That spark of jealousy returned while I jotted down every description he fed me, though an insistent inquiry remained on the forefront of my mind.

Was Maya Mathews a real girl from Brandon's world, one that he was already infatuated with?

He certainly detailed traits that fit the mold for his ideal woman, down to her physical attributes. Wore sophisticated dresses, rather than throwing on casual wear. Did her makeup and hair, presenting herself appropriately. Held intellectual conversations.

As we wrapped up our story, a different thought plagued my mind, one that—unbeknownst to me—would shape the person I was to become. If Brandon truly concocted his ideal woman, I aspired to grow up and become just like this Maya Mathews.

Mia

FOUR YEARS LATER

I EXAMINED myself in the elegant mirror; the finished product was... passable.

My looks fell somewhere in the middle—average—but my makeup was on point tonight, elevating those average traits. The sophisticated dress added a mature touch, as did the designer purse—a gift from Raven—since not many teenagers rocked designer labels.

Glancing at the white nightstand of the small but opulent hotel room, I located the book that had become my lifelong companion. Before leaving the room, I wrapped it carefully in the protective cloth I had purchased—a tad overboard on my part. Anyone to come across it would likely mistake the book for a bible. To me, it might as well be.

Placing it gingerly inside my backpack, I left the room and took the elevator to meet Gabby. I was sharing this room with her, but Gabby was already downstairs.

Gabrielle was a friend of mine who, shockingly, wasn't put off by my… oddities. Her parents invited three of her closest friends and me on a trip to celebrate her eighteenth birthday. They were also staying in this hotel and got us adjacent rooms.

However, this trip served a dual purpose for me. I found out that *he* was coming to the same city, and the dates coincided with Gabby's trip. It had been months since I laid eyes on him, and I was dying for a taste.

"Mia, over here!" Gabby called out when I stepped onto the hotel lobby.

We had a birthday dinner earlier with her parents. Afterward, we decided to change for the nightlife portion of the evening. Our destination—the club adjoined to the hotel via the elongated lobby.

"Hi!"

Gabby gave me a quick hug. "Why are you so late?"

"Sorry, I lost track of time." And took too long in front of the mirror.

"Guess it was worth it." Gabby smacked my butt. She was the kind of person lax about interactions and all sorts of other things, especially boys—making out with someone from hotel security twenty minutes after checking in. "You look like a knock-out."

Actually, Gabby was the real knockout with her golden skin, hazel eyes, and dark hair. The red romper she chose for tonight fit her five-foot-eight frame like a glove. She looked more like a model rather than a future tech wiz.

"Is that cute security guard of yours coming out tonight?" I asked.

"Julien? No." She pouted. "He has to work the surveillance room."

"Too bad."

Gabby led the charge toward the VIP entrance of the club, along with her other friends who stood in line—Avril, Esme, and Priya.

I tilted my head in acknowledgment. "Hey, guys."

Avril smiled tightly. She was the unofficial group leader and quite the head-turner with creamy skin and brown eyes with matching hair.

Esme and Priya were in a deep conversation. They responded in kind with polite smiles.

"We're all here," Gabby moved past them to inform the bouncer. "Table's under Hayford."

"IDs first," he demanded.

The girls reached into their purses while Gabby fished into my mine and dug out a fake ID. She flashed it to the bouncer on my behalf.

I had no intention of ever using that piece of document. Until this very second, I thought Gabby had it made as a joke based on a pseudo name I cherished. Now I realized that this ID had a purpose.

There was an age restriction to enter this club.

The bouncer raised the red velvet rope, handing us over to the hostess. My head moved side to side, scanning the place as we walked to the U-shaped lounge pod.

The girls crammed in, rounding the mahogany table in the middle. Before I followed suit, I took note of how they sat. Their shoulders were pulled back, legs crossed one over the other. I mimicked the pose after sliding in next to Gabby.

My gaze continued to bounce off each corner of the club. Without any sightings, I heavy-heartedly conceded that *he* wasn't here tonight.

However, my surveillance established that our table was receiving the most attention. No surprise there. These girls all looked like models with exotic features and impeccable fashion sense. And for once, my outfit rivaled theirs. Raven picked it out, along with my remaining clothes for the trip.

The same thought must have crossed Avril's mind as one long leg dangled over the other. Legs were Avril's best feature, and she flaunted them tonight with nude pumps. "That dress is... looks expensive." She nodded at my outfit, sounding slightly impressed.

With her arms looped around Avril's, Esme turned in my direction to assess the claim. She was no less striking with caramel complexion and dark, kinky hair, which she had pulled back into a half-up.

"Is that custom made?" she asked, eyes fleeing to her own outfit —black leather tights and a gray top. "It fits well," she acknowledged, though it seemed almost begrudgingly.

"It does," Priya chimed in before I could respond. She also tugged at her outfit—a pencil skirt and a blue crop top that exposed her midriff. "You don't usually wear..." she didn't finish the thought. Tossing her thick dark hair over her shoulders, she asked instead, "Is it new?"

"Yeah. My sister bought it for me."

My heart warmed, realizing Raven thought of a way to protect me even from afar. She had met these girls and anticipated they might be high-strung. I had an inkling that Raven wanted to humble them in a department she excelled in—fashion. She both made and bought me new outfits for this trip.

"I didn't realize you were so skinny, Mia." Avril looked down at her black midi dress that clung tightly to her body. "Totally jealous right now. I have gained like ten pounds since we arrived."

"Actually, you have only gained four pounds since our arrival," I declared right as the other girls vehemently denied Avril's incorrect theory.

"No, you didn't, Av."

"What are you talking about?"

"You're insane. You're so skinny."

An uncomfortable silence befell us as soon as my sentence clashed with theirs.

Avril's eyes widened, mortified. Esme and Priya were shooting daggers in my direction. Gabby bit her bottom lip; her face scrunched up like she needed to mollify a lousy situation.

Unable to understand what was so upsetting, I tracked my actions.

Due to her excessive drinking during this trip and the dates aligning with what I presumed was her menstrual cycle, Avril's belly now had a slight curve that hadn't existed when we first arrived, indicating bloating. Not enough to be ten pounds, but noticeable enough to at least be four or five.

Avril assumed she had gained ten pounds. I was merely informing that she had, in fact, gained *less*.

Surely, that was good news?

Apparently not.

Gabby's friends had never been fans of mine, and my comment sealed the deal. Following the awkward moment, they left me out of their conversations entirely, though Gabby tried her best to include me.

Gabby loved my no-filter tongue, claiming that it made her trust me as I'd never lie to protect her feelings. However, the characteristic she loved the most was my downfall. Her friends, like many others, didn't appreciate my candor, better known as my foot-in-the-mouth syndrome.

My lack of socialization often rendered me clueless. I observed others in order to mimic their social skills, but despite the years of training, my odd cues occasionally slipped out. It wasn't an attempt to be mean, though I doubted I could convince these girls otherwise.

"Finally." Gabby sprang to her feet and clapped her hands with extra enthusiasm, presumably distracting everyone from the tension. "The cavalry is here. Yay!"

Two bottles of vodka, chasers, and glasses were brought to our table, although I ignored the hostess' polite attempt to make me a drink. Gabby's parents had allowed us boundless freedom on this trip since all the girls—minus me—were eighteen. Their one condition was that I didn't drink hard liquor (per Raven's instructions). However, wine, if consumed responsibly, had been approved.

Gabby apparently didn't heed her parents' rules and grabbed one of the vodka bottles. "Okay. We are doing shots. The goal tonight is to finally see *you* drunk."

No way. "I'm good for now."

"You can't say no. It's my birthday."

I quickly stood from my seat. "I have to use the bathroom. Maybe after I come back?" Hopefully, she'd forget about it by then. "Do you know where the restrooms are?"

"It's actually out the way we came, in the hotel lobby."

"Be right back." I scurried away before she could pour the dreaded shots. Plus, I needed a break from the other girls.

On second thought, perhaps I should call it a night altogether rather than force Gabby into the role of a peacemaker on her birthday. I was leaving tomorrow while the rest were staying behind. My absence might as well start now.

Exiting the club, I looked for the restrooms... and stumbled in my heels.

Mussed up inky black hair. Strong set jaw. The palest blue eyes, almost the color of crystals. Couple of sexy tattoos on the outskirts of his index finger. Tasteful enough to give him an edge but small enough to not interfere with his suave attitude.

God! He was so hot.

Brandon Fucking Cooper.

Yes. It was cliché to still be stuck on the same man. If Milo knew of my feelings, he'd have my head. On top of being my brother's business partner and best friend, he was also ten years older than me. He was even older than Milo by a year and a half.

But it was so hard to concentrate on those facts when Brandon was the most perfect specimen to grace this earth. Keeping with his usual air of defiance, he wore a black button-down shirt and slacks instead of a suit like everyone else. And per usual, he was surrounded by a bevy of admirers, further stabbing me deep in my fragile heart.

My glare was steadfast on one particularly pushy girl—another techy entrepreneur whom I recognized from Milo's social circle. She was semi-obsessed with Brandon, much like me. Through my past "stalking," I was aware that Brandon had met her multiple times, though I very much doubted that he so much as recognized her.

God, why did I like him so damn much? He was such a narcissist.

I snorted as she did everything in her power to get his attention. My glower on her was so thick that, for the first time, I fucked up.

I failed to notice that Brandon's attention was locked on me.

The mien on his face left me stumped. Was it possible that I had caught *his* attention?

Perhaps he was simply surprised by this dolled-up version of me. Doubt he would have spared me a second glance if I walked in au natural. Then an unseeing thought crossed my mind.

Brandon Cooper was Drinking. Me. Up.

He pried off the girls fawning over him. Hundreds of scenarios ran through my mind as he made his way over.

Admittedly, I was surprised to find him in the lobby bar instead of the nightclub. During these events, Milo and Brandon generally took potential investors out for a good time.

Before Brandon could walk around the circular bar so I could inquire about it, a douchebag-type thing intruded on our staring competition.

"Hello there."

Brandon stopped in his tracks.

No, I almost shouted, barely repressing my glare at the idiot who ruined the best moment of my life. Brandon Cooper was about to approach *me,* and I so desperately wanted to know what he had to say.

Brandon signaled the bartender for a drink. His gaze was now on this fool, attempting to decipher if he was with me.

"May I buy you a drink?"

My God, was this man still here? "I'm alright. Thank you."

Brandon's eyes never deviated. I gulped, having lost my speech and the power to comprehend my surroundings.

"Oh, come on. Just one drink."

I wanted to slap him across the face.

Sure, I had no future with Brandon, nor would anything transpire between us. But the way he was staring at me... I wanted to experience that lust-driven look just once, to know how it felt to have Brandon Cooper speak to me like I was a woman instead of a little girl.

Was that too much to ask?

Apparently, it was since this man couldn't take the hint. "I really appreciate it, but I'm waiting for someone."

"What idiot keeps a woman like you waiting?"

"I guess that'd be me." Brandon towered over the man, who mumbled meekly, slinking away to the side.

The entire world came to a stop.

Brandon was close enough so I could smell his clean scent, and I... couldn't breathe or move, infatuated.

Kismet!

Mia

BRANDON and I lost contact after the night of my essay competition. Brandon's ego was bruised, and he hadn't spoken to me since.

Distance only elevated my obsession with Brandon. I yearned to learn of his whereabouts so I could "accidentally" show up at the venue. I hated being *that* girl, but after years of obsessing and stalking the same man, I had accepted it without qualms—*I am that girl*.

When I discovered that Brandon attended this event annually, I begged Raven to visit Nice every summer.

A few years ago, Raven moved to Paris for a fashion design program and also to live closer to her parents. Soon after, she started working with her mom. Currently, they run a boutique store together in Paris.

While we weren't blood sisters, Raven and I remained thicker than thieves. Over the last few years, I had spent all of my breaks with her. My home in New York was lonely, devoid of human contact. Whereas France, and especially Raven's neighborhood, gave me life.

That's also how I met Gabby. Her parents were ex-pats as well and lived in Raven's apartment building.

When they invited me on this trip, I realized the dates for this convention coincided with Gabby's birthday. Although my family was wary of granting me freedom, Raven didn't want to deter my budding friendship with Gabby, realizing that my quirky personality didn't leave many socialization opportunities. After speaking with Gabby's parents extensively, Raven indulged me, allowing me to go off with them.

I didn't relish hiding the truth from Raven, but... *Brandon is the one exception to all my rules.*

I asked Gabby if she'd be willing to stay at this hotel. Though she wasn't aware of my little crush, Gabby granted my wish because she was the best.

My seemingly huge victory was dampened when tragedy struck. I heard that Brandon's father passed away recently. Suddenly, it was crucial to see Brandon. He was suffering. I could feel it in my bones and so badly wanted to comfort him even if I could only do so from afar.

And it had to be from afar because a future with him wasn't in the cards.

Though these small peeks into his life satiated my mind, I had been careful about concealing my presence throughout the years. What would have been the point otherwise?

I wasn't dense enough to pursue Brandon, nor would he ever see me in that light. He was out of my league in every way, which was okay for someone like me. Not to mention, my brother didn't want Brandon in my life, and Brandon never fought the injunction.

If I kept popping up unexpectedly, sooner or later, he would have figured out that I periodically stalked him.

But he had caught me red-handed now, and all I could do was gawp like a deer in headlights. Because Brandon was looking at me in a way that he hardly looked at other women—with male interest and tons of it.

The universe had set up this scene perfectly. I refused to miss the opportunity to play out the one fantasy to keep me up at night over the years.

In the story Brandon and I wrote together, our protagonist, Maya Mathews, had also met her love interest at a bar while being approached by another man. When the "hero" of our story saved her, Maya had said, "Finally! I've been waiting for you to come over. What took you so long?"

As I said, kismet.

"You could have come up to me instead," Brandon retorted in that arrogant way of his.

"And miss the chance to watch you intimidate that man?"

Brandon narrowed his eyes. He realized we were playing a role, having similar conversations to the ones we had written for our characters.

"That was... fun," Brandon admitted with a sly smile. "Do you want a drink?"

"That's an affirmative," I replied, repeating the dialogue verbatim.

We presented this story at a competition before Milo banned our... camaraderie. I typed up the story but never threw away our original "manuscript." I had even sewn the vintage parchment papers myself with a handmade cover so it could read like an actual book.

It was my safety blanket and had served as my only companion during the loneliest of nights. Everywhere I went, the makeshift book came with me, and tonight it was safely tucked away in the hotel room upstairs.

It was exhilarating that Brandon Cooper—a self-proclaimed snob who regularly forgot names—recalled a silly story we had written years ago. A story that shaped my life, my personality, my heart. I was a part of his history just like he was a part of mine, and he remembered everything about me.

Others pegged me as overly optimistic of people's shortcomings, but they needed to open their hearts. Brandon's blunt dismissal of frivolous small talk and sarcastic nature made him out to be a jerk. But he wasn't a self-absorbed asshole at all. He was a man of few words and reserved his limited efforts to engage in substantial conversations.

What's so wrong with that?

Brandon valued his time and was simply selective about investing it in those who mattered to him. Somehow, I made the cut.

I was floating on Cloud Nine, but my ecstasy was interrupted by the bartender. "ID, please?"

The play-by-play of our script took a backseat with the cruel reminder of our reality. Brandon appeared visibly embarrassed by the bartender's request, his eyes sweeping over in a hasty motion.

He doesn't want to be seen with someone so much younger.

I wanted the ground to open up and swallow me whole. Unable to take Brandon's regard, I sought out a particular ID from my purse.

Two weeks before our trip, Gabby asked me if I had a preferred alias. I gave her the only name that meant something to me—Maya Mathews. An ID was waiting for me upon my arrival in Nice, courtesy of some sketchy guy from our neighborhood in Paris.

Despite my vow to never use it, I flashed the document to the bartender. Brandon was my one exception for breaking the rules, remember?

Still, I made sure to only order wine. It was legal for me to consume wine in France, so technically, I wasn't doing anything wrong.

Brandon studied the document intently, eyes twinkling. He didn't reprimand me for the fake ID. Brandon wasn't above breaking the rules... or the law. And he knew why I had chosen Maya Mathews as my alias.

Sharing a secret smile, he continued the conversation in the way I had only imagined in my wildest fantasies. I even managed to respond coherently.

The only time our conversation stilted was over my family. I didn't want to ruin this palpable moment by discussing them. The last time my family came into the picture, Brandon had stopped speaking to me altogether. He stopped coming by our house as well.

Leaving behind everyone and everything from home, I redirected our conversation to music, politics, even religion. The night got away from us between the conversations. I could hardly believe this was happening and was even more astonished by Brandon's suggestion at the end of the evening.

"Do you want to come back to my room for a drink?"

I hadn't prepared for this unprecedented request. An invitation to a hotel room generally meant... didn't it?

Perhaps I was reading too much into it.

After all, Brandon seldom showed interest in the female demographic, and only if they were visibly older or upheld his impossibly high standards. He probably didn't want to be alone tonight since his father passed away recently. It couldn't be anything else.

Right?

If Raven were here, she wouldn't see it that way. Raven wanted to shield me from all men and would start screaming at Brandon before dragging me out of this bar. She had voiced her stance on this matter numerous times.

Never go back to a boy's place, especially if you are alone.

But it was difficult to turn Brandon down while surrounded by his signature smell—clean like a rainforest. It was impossible not to feel weak in the knees with this vision of perfection in front of me.

Not to mention, he cared enough to retain every last detail about me. It meant more to me than I could express.

"Sure, I can stay for one more drink."

Brandon left to settle the bill while I texted Gabby about running into a family friend and hanging out with them for the evening—all of which was true.

Out of the corner of my eye, I watched that same woman from earlier, Tasha *something*, sashay over to Brandon. The way I ground my teeth, I'd be shocked if I didn't have to return to the orthodontist for adult braces. I only stopped when Brandon blew her off without a second glance.

My jealousy was quickly replaced by sympathy. Brandon bid her goodnight by calling her the wrong name, despite meeting her numerous times.

Ouch.

Being discarded by Brandon was painful. I could attest to that much.

As sorry as I felt for Tasha, my heart leaped upon Brandon's return with one thought ruling every part of my mind—tonight was the best night of my life.

* * *

It didn't take long for the best night of my life to turn into the nightmare of a lifetime.

I was supposed to be an observant person—someone who rarely missed the small details. But in my obsession with Brandon, I overlooked all the red flags. Blinded by infatuation, I only saw what I *wanted* to see.

Twenty-four hours together, yet I only just realized that Brandon Cooper didn't recognize me.

I wasn't sure exactly when I started to deduce it. There were hints sprinkled throughout. Odd remarks about my family and inquiries about information Brandon should already be privy to.

I kept overlooking it all until... Brandon fucked me.

It wasn't his style to seduce his best friend's younger sister or anyone younger for that matter.

Growing up, I often struggled with reading between the lines and passive-aggressive comments. I understood sarcasm just fine—ingrained into my personality thanks to Brandon—but the rest were a challenge. It made me yearn for a world with straightforward words, one where no one said things they didn't mean.

When Milo noticed my struggles, he gave me a moral compass as a guideline.

Don't get into physical altercations.

If you do something wrong, own up to it.

Let your conscience guide you.

Don't do anything illegal. I didn't, not unless it came to Brandon and my slight habit of stalking.

I knew Brandon thought of me as some naïve good girl. Partly true. I stuck to the path laid out for me and was much too trusting of people's intentions. But contrary to his and my siblings' beliefs, I did possess my own bit of street smarts. And I considered myself strait-laced rather than a good girl.

Clear-cut rules made my life considerably easy. I could blindly follow a set of morals without concerning myself with the profound meanings behind them.

But when Brandon asked me to tag along to Italy, it posed a moral dilemma—my guilty conscience over Milo's reaction warred with leaving a man to mourn the death of his father by his lonesome.

Though I initially resisted the idea, Brandon's grief tore at my soul. Milo had mentioned Brandon's recent loss, my ears perking up to devour every detail he had to spare.

Surely, even Milo would agree that a guilty conscience paled in comparison to a man suffering from loss.

I threw caution to the wind, justifying my action as a one-time deal due to the unique circumstance.

Still, when Brandon made a move, I thwarted his advances,

downright stunned by it. My doubts grew when he progressed further, and my suspicions were confirmed once Brandon moaned the name *Maya* during sex.

My heart cracked open.

It was the first time he had called me by the fictional character's name, sparking a pain like I had never known before. It was humiliating, and I'd barely hung onto my dignity since.

When Brandon finally fell asleep, I stared at my reflection for hours.

The acne from my preteen years had cleared up.

My ugly braces were long gone. Along with it, so was my overbite, entirely altering my smile and facial structure.

My hair was now straight and tamed, courtesy of Raven.

Turning sideways, I also examined my breasts and ass.

I looked like an entirely different person. A grown woman.

Brandon hadn't seen me since I hit puberty. He and Milo hated social media, so probably not even a photo. I couldn't exactly blame Brandon for not recognizing me. It was just a huge fucking insult to be obsessed with someone my entire life who literally didn't remember me, especially since Brandon was infamous for overlooking details about people he didn't care about.

The last realization sucked the most.

Brandon didn't care about Mia with her volatile tendencies, geeky self, and childlike optimism. Whereas he revered the posh Maya with her worldly outlooks and pristine dresses.

At least the dreary predicament led me to a sight I never imagined having the privilege.

Brandon was fast asleep and on full display. The birthday suit did nothing to soften him. Even in sleep, he appeared cruel and harsh... and an undeniable form of male beauty.

I intently studied the man stretched out next to me.

For so long, I had dreamt of having sex with Brandon. Of all the ways I imagined it, this missed the mark. In every one of my fantasies, at the very least, Brandon knew my name. In a freakish nightmare, I was stuck in a world playing the role of a fictional character Brandon was fucking.

Maya Mathews was a character Brandon made up on the worst night of my young life when my mother moved out of our house. The way he had weaved the character—drawing a parallel between me and a descriptive image of his ideal woman—inspired me into that fictional personality.

Whereas Brandon had no recollection of this character, nor did he recognize little Mia, who idolized him. I wasn't even an afterthought to him—just the biggest loser on this planet, nothing more than a borrowed personality.

With a huff, I sat up and reached for the lamp on the nightstand. Allowing my heavy heart to drag, I rose from the soft king-sized bed and grabbed Brandon's button-down shirt. I threw it on and tiptoed toward my oversized purse. Cautiously, I took out the story that started this disaster. This book had calmed me down in the past. Perhaps it'd have the same effect one more time.

I made my way back to the bed and opened the book to read under the dim light. By now, I had memorized every dialogue, every word. Reading it still brought me comfort.

When I felt Brandon shift, I quickly rewrapped the protective cloth over the book, slid it under the bed, and turned off the light. The guilt over betraying Milo—and inadvertently Brandon—was overbearing. I wasn't ready to face him, knowing that come tomorrow, I'd have to confess the truth. I had to bear the torture until then.

I turned over, frantically dragging the comforter with me. Within moments of squeezing my eyes shut, I realized there'd be no sleep tonight.

Brandon felt the movements and reached for me blindly, almost instinctively. With accurate precision, he grabbed my arm and hauled me onto his chest. My face pressed against the taut muscles of his bicep as his hand sifted through the material of the shirt.

I stiffened. "You're awake."

"Who can sleep with your tossing and turning?" he rumbled. "Have you always been a restless sleeper?"

"I get a little tense in new environments..." I trailed off when Brandon peeled my shirt upward to reveal my backside, his hard bulge pressing against my thigh.

"What are you doing?"

"Relaxing your tense muscles."

I closed my eyes. "Go back to sleep."

"I can't. Need a sleeping aid." His palm rubbed the back of my thighs with a gentle caress.

I raised my head and found his eyes open, practically blazing in the moonlight. "I hardly doubt this counts as a sleeping aid."

"It does," he assured. "It's very necessary to feel your bare skin in order to fall back asleep."

"If you're having trouble sleeping, I'm sure we can find you a book to read, or I can make up a bedtime story." The words came out with such laced bitterness that they shocked me. Was this an example of passive-aggressiveness that generally went over my head?

Brandon didn't pick up on the tone or my resentful hint. "Not interested in bedtime stories."

"Then just close your eyes."

"That doesn't work, either. You're the one who woke me up. Help me fall back asleep."

I ground my teeth. "Help yourself."

He tutted. "You talk about religion and being a good Christian. Aren't you supposed to show kindness by helping those in need?"

Before I could retort, he rolled us over, pinning me underneath. His hands landed on the front of the shirt, roughly tearing it open with the buttons scattering in a million directions.

"Brandon," I scolded as the first gust of cold from the air condition greeted my nipples.

He wasted no time. His mouth was on my tip, wet and hot,

standing them to more attention. He twirled his tongue, making me quiver when he hollowed out his cheeks to suck.

"Fuck!" I almost sprang off the bed when he bit the underside of my boob.

He finally stopped, only to move to my other nipple for similar treatment and then once more to take off my shirt completely, leaving me to shiver.

Brandon repeated the process numerous times, sucking, biting, licking every inch of my breasts in turn. He groaned against the meatiest part; my chest dampened from the attention.

"Spread your legs." He gave the instruction but barely waited for me to comply, parting my knees roughly to make space for himself.

"Wait," I said breathlessly. "Protection? We didn't use any before." He had also caught me off guard that first time, so I hadn't thought of it.

His gaze flipped to meet mine for a fleeting moment. "I don't have any, but I'll pull out." Said every man with an illegitimate child.

I frowned.

I might be slightly sheltered, but I had two single brothers. Even without any intention of having sex, what unattached man in his twenties traveled to a foreign land without condoms? This tidbit conflicted with Brandon's otherwise meticulous attitude to shield himself against all odds—reputation, image, women.

Brandon told me he was clean. I believed him. But he shouldn't be risking pregnancies with random women. Just the thought irked me.

However, that Brandon-induced fog trumped all practical considerations. His fingers were between us, stroking my folds while his fully erect dick rubbed against my thigh.

To my horror, my previous irritation over contraception and how the jackass had forgotten about me all but subsided. I squirmed against his hand for friction.

Brandon suppressed a groan, jaw clenching. "I want you wetter," he said throatily, kissing down the length of my body. He bit the side of my torso before moving his mouth to my lower abdomen.

Parting my lips with two fingers, Brandon leaned back to ogle my pink flesh. Modesty shouldn't concern me as I believed the human body to be a beautiful thing. Unease settled in all the same as no one else had seen me naked.

He studied every inch of me like it was a house of worship, chipping away at my hesitancies. Large hands clamped down on the backside of my thighs, raising my knees until my sex was indecently exposed to him.

He placed a swift kiss on my core and murmured against the skin, "Did you like it when I put my mouth on you earlier?"

I swallowed, licking my lips to quench the sudden dry mouth.

He twirled his tongue over my lips, making my legs quake. "Bet I could make your pussy flood."

Raising my head, I stared down. He laughed at my wide-eyed gape, a vindication that he knew I didn't catch his drift.

"I forget how innocent you are." He blew a hot breath over my slit, drawing a shuddering breath out of me.

I watched in bewildered fascination as he lowered his face. My entire body jolted when his wet tongue languidly reached out for a long, slow lick, exploring the entirety of my slit in one motion.

Trembling, I rolled my head backward, head hitting the soft pillow. I bit my bottom lip. The sheets were already damp underneath, my ass cheeks writhing against the wet spot.

And just when I thought I'd be transported to an abyss, his tongue disappeared.

I ground my hips, but all I felt was his hot breath between my legs. Lifting my head, I impatiently peeked down.

His eyes were on mine, playful. "Want to ride my mouth?"

"What?" I squealed, unsure if I heard him correctly.

"I can make you come even harder if you ride my mouth," he mused.

Before I could respond, Brandon wrapped an arm around my middle, rolling me until I was sprawled on top of him. He forced me into a straddle position with sturdy hands while he laid back on the mattress.

My heart slammed against my chest, bravado strained from the daunting task. Brandon was teeming with confidence over his every decision and seemed unwilling to feed into my nerves.

He pulled me forward until I straddled his chest. "I can't wait. Need to feel your wet pussy throbbing in my mouth." There was urgency in his voice and impatience in his eyes.

"Brandon—" I started reluctantly.

He pulled me forward again, this time sliding himself down to align his mouth with my sex.

And then his mouth was on me, this time without holding back.

He lapped vigorously, wet yet with such firm precision that it made my muscles tighten. Brandon's hands closed over my knees and squeezed them closer, trapping his head between my thighs.

The new sensitivity surprised me. With a yelp, I moved. He only gripped me harder, his lewd tongue leaving no stones unturned. My body was flushed from prickling heat, mind delirious.

"God," I sobbed desperately, hands landing on the wall by the head of the bed.

Lips barely detangled from my core as he asked, "Do you love it when I lick you here?"

I gasped, unable to do anything more than nod.

He released one hand to hook it around my thighs and peel my skin upward for more access. "Does it feel good, baby?"

I nodded again, begging with my eyes for him to ease the ache.

His hot breath tickled my slit. "Say it."

"Feels good," I whimpered, and he leaned in for a torturous lick.

"Tell me how much you want this."

"So fucking much." Once again, he only gave me a little of what I needed.

With his mouth on my lips, right outside of where I needed him, Brandon taunted me. My body was ready to shatter, but he planned only to continue if I was vocal. I didn't care. He created the tension, and I needed him to ease it. I'd give him whatever he wanted to release my agony.

"I love it when you lick me."

My back arched as he squeezed my lips together, exposing my clit and sucking viciously. He sucked and licked until my thighs trembled.

"I'm so close. Don't stop. It feels so good."

The taut nerves bunched together, and I stumbled forward, grabbing onto his hair, desperately grinding against his hot mouth.

"Oh," I strained to speak, tears rolling off my cheek. "Oh, God!" I screamed, almost shooting off of him as I exploded.

With a strangled cry, my limp body fell forward, hands landing on either side of his head. Mind numb and depleted, I was floating in a trance when I noticed my limbs were still jerking uncontrollably.

A wet tongue was twirling my wetness around with lazy strokes. Brandon hadn't stopped licking me.

It didn't seem to matter if I had come. Brandon was doing it to please himself rather than me. His eyes were closed, large hands firmly wrapped around my thighs and squeezing, as if loving every second of it.

When he finally stopped, he ended with a small kiss on my clit, releasing his hold on my thighs. I moaned as he slid my dead-weight body down his body, my eyes fluttering but not enough to miss his smug smile.

I was still straddling him with my knees on either side of his body when Brandon guided me to his hips. Grabbing my ass cheeks, he settled me against his hard shaft. Both of our heads were hung low in silent camaraderie as his dick slid between my folds.

"Fuck," he sounded awestruck at the sight, groaning in that earthy throaty way.

So sexy.

So him.

He drew my hips back before he slowly plunged me forward, dragging out a shuddering breath. Inch by inch, he disappeared inside me.

I was dripping wet but couldn't take more of him. I tried to resist, but Brandon rammed in relentlessly with hands on my waist and thighs, even as my entrance threatened to expel the thick girth.

We moaned at the same time as he went deep enough to make my eyes water.

"Fuck, your pussy is so hot and tight around my cock." His head dropped back on the pillow. My fingers clutched at his shoulders for an anchor while his slipped between us. He gave a satisfied growl, lathering them in the slippery mess. "And so wet."

Brandon raised his head to nuzzle my neck. I writhed from the new sensations of this position, hands flat on his chest to steady myself.

"Move your hips," he gritted out agonizingly, "like you did with my tongue."

I shifted but was painfully full of him. With one hand still gripping my waist and the other locked within my folds, he forced me to grind against him, my knees digging into the mattress.

"Yes, like that."

His eyes glowed manically as he watched me, raking over my breasts that were lifting and falling with every effort.

"Fuck yes," he grunted, shifting his hips underneath me in motion.

Encouraged, I moved with him. As I found a steady rhythm, I felt my core tightening once more and dug my nails into his chest. "Oh my God."

His shabby breaths competed with mine, and I could barely hold on. My muscles clenched as he pulsed inside me. I shouted, head thrown back, grappling with ecstasy.

Feeling boneless, I slid forward. Brandon noted the change and rose to the occasion. Removing his fingers from my sex, he firmly gripped my thigh and waist, moving me as he saw fit.

The bed rattled against the wall from his efforts, mattress creaking as he used my body without holding back. I moaned from the aftershocks while he gave out a stifled choke, grinding my hips against him with his large hands until spilling inside me.

He roared, yanking me down to take my lips. I was barely lucid but felt his greedy tongue exploring my mouth without holding back. By the time he pulled back, I could do no more than slump against him.

Brandon wrapped his arms around me.

"You came inside me," I reproached.

He kissed my neck, and I felt his grin against my skin. "Worried that I'll knock you up, then leave to buy a pack of cigarettes and never come back?"

"That's not the point." I did a quick calculation in my head. I'd be in the seventy-two-hour window for Plan B upon my return to Paris.

Brandon sifted his fingers through my hair silently. There was a long pause before he murmured, "Just so you know... I'd take care of you."

I didn't contradict him, irritated. Lifting my hips, I hopped off and shifted over to my side of the bed.

Brandon laughed as if it were cute. "Where do you think you're going?"

Clutching from under my arms, he threw me on top of him like I was meant to be used as his personal throw blanket. He tussled my hair with a satisfied grunt, but it was hardly comfortable sleeping on top of another human being.

"I can't sleep like this."

"You can't sleep either way," he retorted.

Placing my palms flat, I tried to jimmy myself up. In retaliation, his hands landed flat on my shoulder blades to drag me back to his chest.

"Stop," he mumbled. "Tired. Need sleep."

Exasperated, I surrendered. Guess there could be worse places to spend the night than on top of Brandon Stupid Cooper.

* * *

The next day, I lugged around on wooden legs, grappling with the dilemma of how to disclose the truth to Brandon.

In the end, I took the cowardly way out, indulging between the sheets for hours after we returned from the outdoor activities he had planned.

Forbidding as ever, Brandon was sprawled naked on the bed for the second night in a row, having kicked off the covers. Would there ever be anything gentle or sweet about this man?

The moonlight glinted over a set of hard abs so mouthwateringly perfect it made me want to store the image in my reservoir to drool over later. Veins ran down the tanned rippling slopes, stretching onto the ink painted on his torso. Though I had struggled to make it out on both nights, I believed it was a tattoo of an animal of some sort.

Frustrated with another sleepless night, I hopped off the bed and lazily inspected my surroundings. Over the years, I had only seen Brandon in public settings, never in his element and certainly not in his childhood bedroom.

The details of the room surprised me. I always presumed we shared similar interests. Upon closer inspection, it was a wishful fantasy.

The color scheme of the room was ombre. Not my style. His bookshelf—while perfectly respectable—boasted of reading material that wasn't to my taste. Everything was immaculate, orderly, and pristine, opposite of my room.

I walked past his desk, fingers brushing lightly over his personal belongings. An item badgered at my mind enough to do a double-take.

I stiffened mid-step.

The name *Milo Sinclair* was distinctly printed on an official-looking document. Without a second thought, I picked up the stack of papers.

There were multiple contracts pinned together with a paperclip. There was an odd similarity between the documents. When I flipped through them, I realized they were all contracts for divestiture. Contracts Milo had sanctioned.

Why would Brandon carry these around?

Brandon, Milo, Jaci, Alexa, and Asher put up seed money when they started their business. The amount translated into their individual ownership stake. Milo invested his entire trust fund to become the majority owner.

Nevertheless, they needed more capital to turn their beta model into a reality. To gain prospective investors, Milo gave up minuscule ownership ratios throughout the years. These contracts documented each percentage he had forfeited in exchange for capital.

I frowned. It was a hell of a lot more than he should have given up.

"What are you doing?"

I jumped, not expecting Brandon to wake up and catch me with my hand inside the cookie jar. It'd be a blatant attempt to hide my prying if I dropped the papers now. Better to come clean.

"What's this?" I asked, voice lighthearted. I flipped the stack over so he could read the title on the front.

Raising his head off the pillow, Brandon squinted his eyes to view the item in question. "Contracts." He stretched—still naked as the day he was born—and smiled when he caught me staring.

I turned away. "Oh. I didn't realize you were on the clock. Do you have a lot of work to do while we are here?"

His eyes dogged the length of my body, barely covered by another one of his shirts. "Come here." He opened his arm in an invitation.

Dropping the stack of papers, I climbed back into bed. He draped his arms impatiently around my waist to drag me closer. My face landed in the crook of his neck, the clean smell sidetracking my mind instantaneously.

"It's just something I had to look over. But no, I'm not working this weekend." His response surprised me. Brandon never explained himself to others. "So?" His hand slipped under my shirt, idly drawing circles on my bare hips.

The teasing and soft touches turned my brain to mush. I couldn't understand what he was asking of me. "So?"

"So, did you have fun snooping through my shit?"

I would have tensed if the amusement wasn't so thick in his voice. I shouldn't be surprised that Brandon wasn't angry. He didn't lead with anger but rather sarcasm. A refreshing change from us Sinclairs—the hot-headed bunch.

"Just wanted to make sure the man who kidnapped me to Italy wasn't hiding any dead bodies."

"That's a terrible misuse of time. If someone kidnaps you, there is no point searching for proof of their insanity. Instead, you should search the medicine cabinet. If they have any health conditions, you can exploit it."

I smiled. No one could pull off dry humor like Brandon. "And if they don't have any health conditions?"

"They might have other prescription medications. You can either drug them or make them OD on it." His eyes were closed, but he spoke with utmost sincerity.

"Huh. Never thought of that. The only drug in my medicine cabinet is weed."

Brandon stiffened, then raised his head off the pillow. Jaw slightly hanging down, he gaped at me with equal parts of awe and disbelief. "You," he pointed at me, "Ms. Goody Two Shoes, smoke weed?"

"You sound impressed," I mused.

"More like stunned." He paused, then added somewhat begrudgingly, "And a little impressed. At least, you have done one bad thing in your life."

Actually, I have done two bad things.

"Don't be too proud. It's medical marijuana. Prescribed by a doctor and totally legal."

Brandon groaned. "God! You are the only person who manages to make smoking weed sound so fucking lame."

I laughed, throwing my head back.

"Why did they prescribe it?"

I shrugged. "You know, stress, classes, and all that." Plus, it calmed down the stress-induced fits I threw once in a while.

"I'm not surprised that your insane standards and expectations stress you out. It's odd because most of it seems self-imposed."

Brandon's introspective analysis didn't fit the bill with his remaining traits. It was impossible to believe the same man's inattentiveness had landed him in this precarious position with his best friend's little sister.

He met my eyes. "Achieving future ambitions doesn't mean you have to ruin your present."

I said nothing more as Brandon pulled me back to his chest.

My family did have unsurmountable expectations, and I pushed myself to meet them. I was a year ahead in school, starting senior year this fall. The workload led to crippling stress-induced nausea, and I was unable to keep food down for long.

Multiple episodes later, a doctor suggested prescription marijuana since other drugs failed to work. Raven and Reid were for it, while Milo loathed all drugs with a passion. This was the point of a long-standing argument, even though meditation and prescription marijuana had turned me onto a better path.

"Answer this question without thinking," Brandon spoke

suddenly. "If you could do anything or be anyone, what would it be?"

"A makeup artist," I answered without hesitation. "And I'd want to create a clean line of products by making my own."

"Clean products?"

"Like vegan makeup."

Growing up, Milo and I shared a bond over our mutual passion for academics. He encouraged me to compete with him in trivia and political discussions and was never displeased if I bested him. If anything, he spurred me on.

However, our opinions varied on the application of said academics. Milo was ambitious and driven. He loved applicable knowledge with the means to better our lives. Whereas I loved knowledge for the sheer sake of learning.

I was interested in human behavior because of my mom and because I could never master it myself. Milo pegged it as my calling and identified the best undergraduate programs for Psychology—Stanford and Yale.

Yale won because it was closer to home.

I was too young to understand the weight of his dreams for me—a Park Avenue home, a title in front of my name, respect, adoration, an all-around good life. He simply forgot to ask if that's what I wanted.

By the time I had developed my own interests, I was already in too deep. None of what I wanted fit the bill for what Milo had in store for me.

Milo was the golden child, and he expected me to be even better. I didn't have the heart to disappoint the brother who traded in his own childhood in exchange for mine. It seemed awful to become a starving artist after all he had given up for my sake. In return, he only wanted a good life for me so he could rest easy. Who was I to deny him so little?

Besides, it seemed logical based on my skill sets. Anyone around me for five minutes also assumed I'd pursue something academia-oriented.

I waited for Brandon to voice similar opinions.

"Interesting concept. But getting to that point should hardly be so stressful that you need a prescription to function."

I peeked up at Brandon, surprised that he *wasn't* surprised. His devastatingly handsome face was solemn, devoid of any personal opinions. He had no expectations out of me other than whatever I wanted in life. It was… beautifully liberating.

"You're right. It shouldn't."

Brandon grabbed my hand, thumb gently stroking it in soothing motions. I stared at our intertwined fingers, wondering for the hundredth time if now was the opportune moment to come clean.

Please don't hate me.

Brandon spoke before I could open my mouth. "There is something you should know about my family."

Grieving over his dad had opened up slivers of Brandon's heart. I knew it was temporary. As soon as he healed, Brandon would return to his reserved self. But in the interim, I sought to soak up all he had to share.

However, I had lost the right to hear his innermost thoughts as Brandon would be sharing it with a fictional character—a fake woman—not me.

"Brandon, I know it's difficult for you to speak about your family. You don't have to talk about it."

"I don't *have* to," he agreed, "but I *want* to."

My face rested in the crook of his neck, ear pressed against his chest. I could hear his heart racing. Brandon was nervous. A first.

"Years ago, there was a scandal surrounding my family. Dad eventually buried the stories with money, so you can't find this information online; it only exists in the form of hearsay. But I wanted you to know the truth about me. My dad… cheated on my mom with an underaged girl."

I froze.

Brandon also paused for a few beats, assessing my reaction. "Carmen was one of my best friends and only seventeen when their affair first started. She lied about her age. By the time Dad found out, he was already in too deep and refused to break it off. It's the reason why I was so angry with him."

I had the sudden urge to throw up.

"Carmen used to joke how she never wanted to work a day in her life and would much rather trap a rich older man than attend college. I blew it off. Thought it was funny. Never in a million years did I think she'd trap *my* father and destroy our family in the process. I fucking hate her for it."

He rested his chin on my temple, stroking my hair.

"Everyone thought the apple didn't fall far from the tree and had this prejudice against me. They didn't understand; it made me sick to think of what he did. I'd never do that. *Ever.*"

If only he knew.

This was the most Brandon had shared in my lifetime. I used to get giddy whenever he opened up even a little. And now, I wished he hadn't. If Brandon could see my expression, he'd notice the mortification written on my face.

"The whole experience left me... jaded. For so long, I lived my life disproving everyone else and their gossip. Always feeling suspicious of women and their intentions."

He cupped my chin to tip my face, spearing me with a vulnerability I had never seen on him before.

"But I'm trying really hard to be different and not let my past affect things between us," he added quietly.

Brandon smiled sadly when I didn't speak. If it were anyone else, I would have believed he was searching for reassurance. But I couldn't have formulated a response had I tried.

I had never heard this story before, nor had I come across this information. Not surprising. I stalked Brandon by visiting locations he frequented rather than digging into his past.

Everything finally clicked. There was a reason Brandon only pursued older women on the rare instances he gave the female demographic any attention. He was fighting against preconceived notions.

For years, I was happy to peek into Brandon's life from a safe distance. Why did I make the mistake of interacting with him? In one weekend, I ruined everything he had built to protect his reputation.

It wasn't bad enough that I had inadvertently deceived him. Now I had to conceal it too. Brandon was struggling with his dad's death and family history. If he found out my identity, he'd be repulsed, both by himself and me.

All this time, I had justified this trip as a special circumstance because Brandon lost his dad. I never meant to put him in jeopardy.

This damage was irreversible. An underaged girl had lost her virginity to Brandon. And in my attempt to join Brandon in Italy, I fabricated a whole narrative for Raven. I begged her to let me extend the trip. Meanwhile, Gabby told her parents that I had left for Paris.

Until my flight out, I had nowhere else to go.

So, there was nothing more to it except blocking everything else out and living out the remaining days with the fantasy I'd never otherwise experience. After that, I'd ensure no one found out about what happened between us. And never again would I show my face to Brandon.

Part of me died a thousand times at just the thought.

Chapter 14

Mia

My back strummed against the wall, wrists painfully bruised from Brandon's hold. Hot breath tickled my cheek. I dared not face him, worried about my own reaction if I acknowledged him.

Brandon insisted we couldn't make our flight out from Nice due to a malfunctioning rental car. Something about it nigged at the back of my mind, especially as he throttled every one of my alternate suggestions.

"There are no train stations in a hundred-mile radius," Brandon had chewed out.

The statement confirmed my theory. We passed both the town center and a train station on our way to the cottage. It dawned on me that Brandon had fabricated our limitations.

Brandon was stingy with his words, so I generally read his body language to decipher his thoughts. But today, he was giving nothing away. Stoic face, blank eyes, nonexistent body language.

But his manipulation and motives were the least of my concerns. I was far more anxious about returning home. If I missed my flight,

Raven would gather a search party stretching all of Europe and undoubtedly uncover my link to Brandon in the process.

I tried to make Brandon see reason, but he wouldn't budge.

"I'm not trying to keep you here," Brandon had repelled my accusation at some point. "I'll get the damn car fixed. Until then, I don't want to keep having the same discussion because there is nothing more I can do. You've clearly been sheltered your whole life and don't know how to deal with unexpected predicaments. Sometimes shit happens that's out of our control. It's part of life, so get a goddamn grip on yourself."

The comment hit a little too close to home, provoking the anger I had been masking around him because Maya didn't succumb to anger so easily.

However, Mia... now she was a beast of her own.

Unable to keep up the pretense any longer, I blurted out, "Go to hell, Brandon! I'm leaving, even if I have to walk back to Nice. I'm sure I'll find another man who'll be happy to—"

My sentence was cut off by Brandon shoving me against the wall. Hard. He hadn't moved from the position since, his larger frame blocking any chance of escape.

Shaken to my core, I averted his gaze. It was the first glimpse of violence Brandon had displayed. At most, he sneered and taunted rather than getting angry... until now.

I had promised to fake it until we amicably parted ways. I should have known better. This was the only way it could have ended—an explosive blowout. Expecting differently was plain naïve.

I was straight edge, following the course set for me. Brandon was the tornado to obliterate it all. This obsession with him had cost me dearly throughout my life because I broke every rule at my disposal for him.

He was my motivation to lie and do things I'd never otherwise do. Brandon was the reason for the first time I skipped school. As a result, I got stuck in a walk-in freezer and lost the privileges of sharing a home with my mother. I lied to Raven about this trip, only to lose my virginity to a man who didn't so much as remember my name.

I had no one to blame other than myself. Brandon turned me into a bumbling idiot because I allowed it. Despite my attempts to act older, these moments made me face the harsh reality of things.

I was only sixteen and petrified of the man in front of me, the one I was stuck with while in the middle of nowhere.

I gently placed my hands on Brandon's chest to give him a mild push, but he only leaned into me more. Disregarding my tentative struggles for escape, he deliberately crushed me against the wall. I felt his urgent need budding with the erratically beating heart under my palm and the hard bulge against my stomach.

To my horror, Brandon leaned in to kiss me. I turned my face away. "I shouldn't have said that," I quickly whispered. Whatever it took to appease him.

"No, you shouldn't have."

With a stern glare, his eyes moved over my face, though he didn't let me go. As if impelled purely by instinct, he buried his face in my hair and inhaled deeply, sounding overwhelmed by the smell. With each one of his exhalations, he verged on more madness.

The scent of rainforest filling my lungs failed to have the same effect on me. Instead, the warmth of him wrapped tightly around me in a chokehold. Brandon was a man possessed, staring at me with nefarious intentions. Like I was his to consume. And all I could do was stare at the far corner of the room with blank eyes, wishing for this nightmare to end.

Similar thoughts must have crossed his mind. Or perhaps it was the dread written on my face, pleading eyes begging silently. Whatever his reason, Brandon picked up on the cue and snapped out of it at long last.

"I'll take the car into town to see if they can fix it," he said without moving.

Our gazes collided, breath fanning against one another. Suddenly, he grabbed my jaw and kissed me with such absorption that my knees banged against one another. I clung to him for dear life as his hot mouth devoured mine. With hands that might have been slightly trembling, he shaped and squeezed my breasts, which rose and fell in response.

When he pulled back, our ragged breaths intermingled. With hazy eyes still fixed on my lips, Brandon panted harshly. His rapid blinking could only indicate he was clearing his vision while regaining lucidity.

He detangled at an agonizingly slow pace. It appeared that the control was causing him every bit of the torment etched on his face. Walking backward, he turned away from me to grab the car keys. Brandon opened the front door, slamming it shut after him, the sound loud enough to vibrate through my insides.

It took minutes to regain my faculties and the feel of my puffy lips to return. The confinement he left me in while he was "fixing the car" jarred my panic, but I had to disregard it. I needed to act fast to get out of this predicament.

Brandon left me captive in this cottage, thinking the place was too remote for an escape. That wasn't necessarily the case.

Though it took us forty-five from the city center to this cottage, it was likely due to the twisted roads—uphill and downhill. I doubted the actual distance was more than a mere ten miles.

And ten miles on the road didn't equate to the same in nautical time.

If I had to guess, there was a ferry nearby for the local residents. Their lives were water-based, and that long, twisted road didn't serve the purpose of an efficient means of commuting day-to-day, especially if they worked in the city center.

Tapping on the off-line map on my phone, I noted that the city center did, in fact, connect to water.

This cottage was also near water.

When Brandon and I walked to the beach to scatter his dad's ashes, there were boats and fishermen in the distance. I could flag one of them down and offer them money in exchange for a ride to the ferry. My Google Translate app worked offline in case they only spoke Italian.

Without hesitation, I threw my belongings into my carry-on, packing all other essentials into my oversized bag. Fifteen minutes had already elapsed since Brandon's departure, and I still needed to erase all traces of my existence.

Brandon didn't know my identity, and I couldn't risk exposing it. He already knew of my little crush. So, it'd be too much of a coincidence all of this happened under the guise of a misunderstanding. He'd hate me if he found out the truth and would accuse me of premeditating everything, just like his stepmother.

I searched every crevice of the house to ensure none of my personal belongings were left behind, scrambling like a madwoman. My stomach lurched upon realizing that I had almost left behind my most precious possession.

Dashing through the open living room, I got down on my hands and knees to retrieve my book from under the bed. While on all fours, something else caught my eye.

I was at eye level with Brandon's duffel bag. A small square box stood stoutly between the unzipped opening. My fingers hovered over it before I realized it was a box of condoms.

I gritted my teeth, wanting to tear my hair out.

He was such an asshole!

Suppressing the urge to scream, I checked for damages before tucking the book inside my purse.

Brandon had pointed out a fancy pager used to call their groundskeeper. I paged him, hoping he'd polish this place clean.

It was drastic, but so was Brandon at the moment. Coping with loss had altered his perception. He'd rather remain in this cottage to evade reality, something I simply couldn't afford.

After his grief had lapsed, Brandon would forget all about this weekend, and just like he had before, he'd forget me all over again.

* * *

I doubted my journey to Nice would be as smooth as the one to the town center. A fisherman saw me waving frantically from the beach and was nice enough to give me a ride in his boat to the nearest dock. The twenty-minute ferry ride into town was fairly quick. Upon arrival, another nice gentleman pointed out the train station.

Though it was implausible to catch a direct train to Nice from this remote village, my phone had signal at long last.

Milo had a tracking app installed on my phone. Luckily, it didn't work overseas. As far as he was concerned, I was with Raven. And Raven didn't expect me to check in with her until tomorrow.

So, I only had one person to call.

I pressed on Gabby's name as I trudged my carry-on along. "Hey."

"Mia!" she squealed. "Tell me every—"

"Gabby, I need your help," I cut her off, hoping she could hear the panic in my voice.

I gave Gabby a recap of my weekend, leaving out all the sordid details. Instead, I stressed that Brandon and I couldn't be linked together for a few morally reprehensible reasons.

I was especially paranoid of the people who bore witness to us—the bartender, a man who hit on me, and Tasha *something*.

"Mia," Gabby cooed. "I doubt some drunk creep at a bar will remember you. As for the bartender, there were so many people at the hotel that night. How could he possibly remember one random girl?"

"But he checked my ID."

"Doesn't matter. All the information on it is fake. It's not linked to you."

"That's true," I admitted.

I was being overly paranoid, but it couldn't be helped. If Brandon weren't grieving and didn't try to deliberately trap me, I wouldn't be covering my bases in this manner.

"Still, what if he took a photo of me while I wasn't looking? All he has to do is show it to one person. And these hotels have security cameras in the lobby. If he thinks of pulling the footage, how hard would it be—"

"Mia, calm down," Gabby cut off my escalating voice. "Take a breath."

"It could happen," I said in a small voice. Farfetched, yes. But not out of the realm of possibilities.

She sighed. "How about this? Julien told me that the hotel security tapes malfunctioned the other day, and two days' worth of footage got accidentally wiped out. What if it were to happen again?"

"You'd ask him to do that for me?" I hated the idea of putting Julien's job in jeopardy, but I couldn't trample my relief over Gabby's latest fling working in hotel security.

Gabby laughed. "At least something good should come out of one of us hooking up with a cute boy."

Despite Gabby's assurances, I remained unconvinced of getting away with it so easily. "But what about Tasha? She looked right at me that night."

"Tasha is trickier," she slowly admitted. "Have you guys officially met?"

I shook my head before realizing Gabby couldn't see me. "No. I've only seen her at Milo's parties." And the times I stalked Brandon. "I have no idea if she recognized me."

"Alright, let me see what I can do."

Gabby was a mastermind, and I was eternally grateful for it. By the time I found the train station and booked a ticket to the next transfer point, Gabby texted to assure me that she had cornered Tasha at the hotel. Tasha wouldn't say a word about me or anyone else matching my description. And all the security footage was history.

With a final sigh of relief, I let the rocking train lull me into slumber. I had barely evaded disaster and vowed to myself that I had been scared straight and was done stalking Brandon Cooper.

I had always presumed he was misunderstood like the Wicked Witch of the West. Wished I had preserved *that* image of him.

Instead, I met him in person and ruined the memories of Brandon, my friend. If I could go back in time, I would have never followed him to begin with. Would have turned around long before setting foot in that bar and reminded myself of the snippets of dark traits I had borne witness to over the years.

* * *

"What the hell, Brandon?" Liz screamed as soon as she walked through the door. She looked pretty in her long dress. Really pretty.

It was prom night, and something called an after-party was being held at the split-level apartment. Milo would be angry if he found me here, but he was busy arguing with Reid outside. So, once the nanny fell asleep on the couch, I snuck in because I wanted to tell Brandon what I had learned about climate change today. He told me not to look at the internet anymore.

Brandon and I sat side by side on the couch as Liz charged toward us. She was one of Milo's friends and really nice. But I could tell she was different tonight. There were tear stains on her cheeks, and she was upset.

When she neared, I balled myself to the opposite end of the sofa.

Brandon glanced at her. "Nice to see you too, Liz."

"NICE TO SEE YOU?" she screamed. "That's all you have to say after you ditched me and didn't respond to any of my calls or texts? You're such an asshole."

Brandon nodded at me. "We have an eight-year-old in our mix tonight. Might want to watch the language."

I was nine, but of course, Brandon forgot. Again.

Not to mention, he cursed in front of me all the time.

Liz's eyes met mine and softened. "Oh, hi, Mia."

I gave her a meek wave in response.

Maybe, I should have left, but I had developed a terrible habit of listening to other people's conversations. I knew it was bad, but no one ever told me things. It was the only way to find out what was happening around me.

That's how I overheard Raven warning Liz against asking Brandon to prom. She said Brandon wasn't the kind of guy who called girls or made plans, and he only showed up if he felt like it. Liz didn't take the advice, and now her prom was ruined.

She turned back to Brandon and whispered, "Why? What did I do wrong?"

Brandon closed his eyes and rubbed his temples. "To be honest, prom's not my thing. This is more my speed." He gestured around the room.

Brandon was lying.

He was barely paying attention when Liz asked him to prom. At first, he said no. After she pressed a few times about going as friends, he said 'fine.'

Sometimes Brandon said yes to people so they'd stop bothering him. He didn't like being nagged and had done things like this before. I bet he forgot about the date and came straight here without giving her a second thought.

Liz looked sad. "You could have just told me that instead of blowing me off. Why didn't you bring me here with you?"

Brandon lifted a shoulder. "Looks like you still made it here by yourself."

I cast him an irritated look. I hated that Liz liked him, but what Brandon did was mean.

One time, Mom and I went shopping. At some point, she forgot about me and wandered away. I waited for hours and was in hysterical tears by the time a frantic Milo came looking for me. Apparently, Mom couldn't remember where she saw me last and called him in a panic. He searched every store in the mall before finding and pacifying me.

Afterward, Milo was so angry that he refused to speak to Mom for weeks. Milo could hold grudges like no one else, and to this day, Mom wasn't allowed to take me places without his permission.

Milo was Mom's favorite, so the whole situation made her sad. But I understood his anger. It sucked being left behind. No one should do that to you.

Liz's bottom lip trembled. "I should have never asked you to prom. Everyone told me to stay away from you. I should have listened."

Brandon's eyes flipped to Liz's again, bored. "Yeah, probably."

Shaking her head, Liz stormed off.

I stood from the sofa as well.

Confused, Brandon glanced at me. "What? You are done telling me all about the melting ice."

"I should go upstairs before Milo comes back." For the first time, I didn't feel like telling Brandon about what I had learned. And for the first time, I feared Milo might be right.

Brandon wasn't a nice boy.

SIX MONTHS LATER

Brandon

Milo didn't approve of spending my day stationed at the bar, getting drunk. Mr. Responsible devoted his time taking notes like a good little trooper. He even declined to join me for a fucking drink afterward.

God, that guy was insufferable.

Some people were happy drunks. Not me. Everyone pissed me off when I drank, especially while left to drink alone.

This shit was depressing.

I found myself looking up at the entranceway every fifteen seconds, knowing it was unlikely for a certain blonde-haired girl to walk through those doors. Still, I glanced up like clockwork for yet another disappointing—

What.

The.

Fuck.

I froze in place, accidentally spilling my drink on the bar counter. Through the entranceway, I could see the hotel restaurant and... Maya.

She was standing there... hugging Milo.

* * *

Mia

"Just think about it," I pressed, unable to conceal my eagerness. We loitered outside of the hotel restaurant, following the early dinner.

Milo suspiciously narrowed his eyes. "I don't understand why you have been so interested in my company lately."

I shrugged nonchalantly. "Remember when you sent me your company by-laws for my econ project? I researched the potential of reaching IPO for companies that do micro-investments. It might make sense to have big players as investors, but down the road, each percentage you give away could mean another million."

My face was placid though I felt irritated that I couldn't disclose to Milo how I had come across this information and what had sparked my concerns.

When I was at the cottage with Brandon, I came upon divestiture contracts and realized Milo had sold too much of his company. I hadn't been able to hold back my tongue and, over the last few months, had taken every opportunity to warn him against it.

The efforts were futile. Who could blame him for not heeding a teenager's opinions regarding a multimillion-dollar company?

Milo sighed. "Fine. Guess I could ask Brandon to pull up the contracts since it's only the hundredth time you've brought it up. But I doubt he can access the files from here."

I froze.

"W-What?" I blinked, certain that I had heard him wrong. "Here? Brandon's here? In Nice?"

Milo nodded. Meanwhile, it took everything in me not to gasp.

This convention in Nice took place twice a year—summer and winter. Typically, Brandon attended the summer convention while Milo took the winter session.

This year, the convention took place shortly after New Year's. Milo flew me out, intending to make a vacation out of it. We were staying here during the convention, along with the subsequent weekend. He rarely had the time to indulge in vacation, so I was elated by the offer.

I wouldn't have agreed if I knew Brandon was here.

After returning to New York, I had kept my vow and didn't keep tabs on him anymore. But I had also been vehemently cautious against running into him.

My paranoid eyes swept the surroundings. "But I thought you were coming to Nice alone," I reproached.

Milo frowned. "I did. Brandon only flew in today. Why does it matter, anyway? You used to love Brandon. I was the one who didn't like his influence on you." He shrugged. "Assumed you'd be happy to see him after all this time."

I browsed my setting, struggling to find a reasonable excuse now that Milo no longer believed Brandon to possess the capacity to corrupt me. "I-I just thought you wanted to spend time with *me*."

"I do," Milo replied patiently. "Brandon being here doesn't change that."

It changes everything.

"But this vacation was supposed to be only the two of us."

"It is. I doubt we'll even see him." Milo nudged his head toward the bar where Brandon had once caught me ogling him. "He hasn't even left that godforsaken bar since he arrived."

My back stiffened.

Brandon is less than fifty feet away.

Unable to focus on the conversation any longer, I stammered, "Oh-Oh, okay. Think I'm going to head back to my room."

"Alright." Milo eyed me carefully. "I still have one more meeting. I'll come by to check on you after."

Remaining impassive, I simply nodded and bid Milo a hasty goodbye with a hug. My heart raced, heels clicking against the marble floor while making quick footwork toward my hotel room.

An invisible cloak prickled my senses as if someone was following me. Hastily, I kept my gaze forward. I was being paranoid. If someone were behind me, I would have heard their footsteps by now.

I swiped the key card against the pad of my door and this time felt cocooned into an embrace, heat enveloping my back. My breath caught, blinking at the unfamiliar sensation before the sound of deep breathing reached my ears.

I turned quickly and barely caught a glimpse of the palest blue orbs before I stepped backward, and the door fell open.

Brandon.

Without a word, he followed me inside the room.

Brandon didn't appear normal, more like a torn-down version of his former self. A ruffian with the new five o'clock shadow he sported, tousled hair, and red-rimmed eyes. The hypnotizing crystals gleamed for a horrifying moment.

I was aware of how close we stood and could see the muscles flexing under his shirt. Face carved with fury, his larger-than-life stature loomed over me menacingly. "Fuck," he muttered.

I had hoped for a different scenario when the ruse was up. In the best-case scenario, I had hoped it'd be on my death bed.

In the worst-case scenario, we'd run into each other years down the line after he had forgotten what I looked like.

Instead, it had only been six months, and the wound was much too fresh. He might be angry over my identity, but he had hurt me just as badly.

"Mia?" His mien was incredulous.

"You don't remember me, do you?" I asked softly.

"You've..." he looked me up and down, "...changed."

Yes, I changed. But still, he didn't recognize me at all, not even a little?

"I realized who you were when I saw you with Milo," he added.

For several moments, he said nothing more before the shock subsided and a different conflict dawned on him.

"How old are you?" he asked, slow and cautious in his dialogue.

"I turned seventeen a couple of months ago."

His head snapped back, mind reeling. He was calculating my age the first time we had sex. I was sixteen at the time, perfectly legal in France.

"We didn't do anything illegal," I quickly added.

Brandon seemed far from reassured. He ran two hands through his hair and breathed heavily, sweat beads forming on his temple. I knew where his mind had fled—his dad. To him, history was repeating itself in the most horrifying way. The guilt hung heavily on his face.

There was a burning desire to console him, to unburden him of this guilt. My hand reached out for him. "Brandon..."

"You're just a kid." He rubbed his temples with repressed disgust in his voice.

My hand fell away, dejected eyes dropping to the floor. Perhaps by law, we didn't do anything wrong, but it was still way too fucked up.

"You were even younger when we first..." he couldn't finish the sentence. "Just sixteen... Fuck. Fuck. Fuck."

He paced the length of the room and cursed some more.

Brandon looked distraught while he ran two hands up the sides of his head.

"I have known you since you were a baby ...." Brandon paced, interlocking his fingers above his crown. "Babysat you. The things we did... Fuck." He put the heel of his palm on his forehead as if erasing the memories.

Brandon wasn't himself. There was no dry sarcasm, and his cool veneer had shredded into a million pieces. I was staring at a stranger rather than a man I had known my entire life.

Again, I wanted to reach for him, but an invisible barrier separated us.

Brandon hated his father for this exact reason, and now he hated himself for having gone down the same path. Suffering Milo's wrath and risking his reputation paled in comparison to his personal dilemma.

He shook his head with a self-deprecating smile. "I spent years hating him. Now, I'm even worse than my father. How fucked up is that?"

"Brandon, no—"

He whirled around, leaving my mouth hanging in mid-sentence. "I didn't recognize you, but you must have recognized me. Why did you lie to me?"

Just as I had feared, Brandon was accosting me upon finding out the truth. *He is repulsed by me.*

"I didn't lie," I said carefully. "I thought w-we were acting."

"Excuse me?"

"Playing out the roles from that story we wrote," I explained, unable to hide the hopefulness that had crawled into my tone.

His features tensed. "What are you talking about?"

I searched his face for any sign of recognition. When nothing sparked, my disappointment hung heavier than ever. *How can he still not remember?*

I quietly turned toward my unruly suitcase. It lay dormant on a chair next to the fireplace, which the hotel staff had turned on earlier. There was protective glass on either side of the fire. Only the top was left open, adding cozy heat during the cold month along with extra illumination to sort through my disheveled luggage.

Clothes and shoes spilled out of my burgundy carry-on. Under any other circumstance, Brandon would have given me a stern lecture about it.

Sorting through the mess, I pulled out the book, removing the protective cloth on top. For years, this book had been for my eyes only, though technically, Brandon was a part-owner.

Impatient for answers, Brandon moved to stand next to me, and I reluctantly handed the book over. "Here."

He looked down at the makeshift book fashioned out of parchment papers with poorly sewn strings. "What the hell is this?"

"Open it."

"I don't need to read a book. Use your damn words to explain."

"It'll be self-explanatory if you just open it," I insisted softly.

Brandon snatched the book from my hand and opened it roughly. My heart twisted at his careless attitude. It was hard to watch my prized possession be handled with utter negligence.

"Careful," I couldn't help but implore. "It's fragile. I don't know why we wrote this story on parchment paper." I laughed nervously. "It took forever to put it together."

He didn't respond, eyes glossing over the pages. Horizontal stripes of shadows from the fire highlighted his face, allowing me to see his reaction. The veil had lifted by the way Brandon rubbed his scruffy beard. The book wasn't very long, and by the last page, comprehension had settled.

"It was for that essay competition," I reminded.

Brandon slowly lifted his head, eyes dripping with disbelief. "Are you fucking kidding me?"

What?! "I-I thought we were playing a role because you went along with those dialogues."

Surely, he must realize this was all a cruel misunderstanding. It wasn't planned.

"You planned all of this," he accused. "No one in their right mind would remember some stupid story from almost five years ago. I can't even remember who I met *yesterday*, but you clearly did." He pointed at the book. "And you used it to trick me."

My eyes widened at his harsh and slightly unfair accusation. My worst crimes against him were showing up to places he frequented. Okay... and stalking him a little. But despite my feelings, I never made contact.

Technically, Brandon pursued *me*. He pushed me at every turn. I fought the injunction because I understood the ramifications of those actions. Even while together, I never let myself believe it could be more.

Brandon moved closer, watching me suspiciously as he geared up to something cruel. He raised the book, holding it next to his face. "I basically gave you access to my thoughts. And what, you wanted to play it out in real life? Manipulate me with that information?" he accused, voice thick with revulsion.

My bottom lip quivered because it was slightly true. I knew Brandon's likes and dislikes, his humor and conversation preferences, the type of clothing he loved on a woman, even down to what he had wanted to hear while scattering his dad's ashes.

Subconsciously, I had suppressed my personality, painting the image of a woman he'd prefer. But it was registering to me that perhaps none of what we had shared together was real because that person wasn't me.

My only saving grace? It was unintentional. I had no ulterior motives to manipulate him.

"I swear, I wasn't *trying* to trick you," I whispered gravely. "You were sad about your dad... and then you asked me to come with you to Italy. I thought you knew who I was. It was a misunderstanding."

"Even so, you must have realized at some point that I didn't recognize you."

"Yes, but—"

"Then why didn't you come clean?"

I wrapped my arms protectively around my middle. How could I explain it to him? I should have come clean, but I felt cornered after Brandon disclosed about Carmen.

"That's what I thought. This is exactly why I never trust anyone," he said bitterly. "How could you drag me into this? It's sick." His husky voice did nothing to erase the viciousness in his tone.

"Please, stop," I protested, upset. "Even if you think I did this to create some crazy fantasy—which I didn't—deep down, you know that I'd never do anything to intentionally hurt Milo. Nothing and no one comes before him."

Brandon's eyes widened. Some realization he hadn't considered until this very moment seemed to dawn on him. And it appeared to be the icing on the cake.

"That's too bad because Milo's the one who turned you into a brat over the years," he shouted. "Entitled. Little. Brat. Doing whatever you feel like. You never think of the consequences, do you, *Maya*?"

I stilled.

Brandon was grieving after his dad's death and in search of solidifying a human connection. So, he tried to trap me in every possible way. He pushed me into sex, refused to use protection, came inside me on purpose, and misled me about the car.

He didn't think I'd figure all of that out?

Given the magnitude of the situation and his anguish at the time, I could let all of those things go. Grief could make people act out of control.

Blindsided by these current events, he needed a moment to

process and react. He even overlooked the part he played, taking zero accountability. Fine. I could accept this, too.

But calling me by *that* name...

Rancid wrath that knew no bounds flew through my veins. My ears burned, nose flaring. My rage had come into the mix, spiking with his every accusation.

"My name is Mia!" I ground out.

Brandon glowered, uncaring that he had referred to me by *that* name.

"And I might have dropped the ball on coming clean to you, but you were just as responsible for this mistake between us," I added angrily.

His lips curled at my rebuttal. "Well, *Mia.* I'll hand it to you. Considering how much of a mistake it was, you screamed like it was real."

"Well, it wasn't," I seethed, unthinking. "Nothing about a fictional character or their actions are real. I'm not *her*. *She* doesn't exist. It might as well have been a hallucination that you conjured inside your head."

It was an impulsive response. Like a compulsion, my words had toppled out because I hadn't been able to help myself.

Still, it seemed harsh.

Something resembling a wounded expression crossed Brandon's face. Only for a nanosecond, though. After that, hard lines set in its place. Jaw ticking, Brandon glared at the fireplace heating the room.

I considered retracting my words when he spoke. "If I hadn't taken pity and helped you, you could have never used this against me. But you're right about one thing that I had refused to admit until now." He looked me straight in the eyes. "It wasn't real."

Shards of tiny ice made irreparable cracks in my heart. Something awful was about to happen. I could feel the premonition written in his fierce scowl. I took a step forward to mollify him, but it was too late.

Brandon lowered his eyebrows—and perhaps there was a flicker of hesitation—before he raised his hand over the fireplace opening and threw my book into the fire.

* * *

"No." I propelled forward, but it was too late.

The parchment papers burnt to a crisp, taking with it the soul I had poured into them. The flames ate the pages that had saved me on countless nights. When the loneliness became unbearable, I'd take this book out and read it to myself, envisioning the way Brandon had once read it.

It was my only solace in a house that was otherwise pin-drop silent.

"Why?" I asked stoically.

"Because you need to grow the fuck up and stop believing in fairytales."

My brothers weren't big on displaying emotions, nor were my parents. I was no stranger to cold dismissal, but Brandon took the cake for not having a care in the world. He felt no sympathy for my heartbreak, his rage suffocatingly overpowering.

I always assumed Brandon was misunderstood, so I would perpetually give him the benefit of the doubt. I shouldn't have.

Brandon was evil.

I stood motionless, watching my very essence go up in flames. It was so quiet in the room that I could hear how in every last way the pages burned, each sound descriptive of the gashes left behind on my heart.

Once the horrific task was over, so were my emotions.

I had the tendency to act brashly. However, I was determined against it. Instead of reacting, I calmly walked to the door and held it open.

"Get out," I ordered.

A couple in the hallway passed the open door and turned their heads to make direct eye contact with us.

"Get out before I start screaming and someone calls security." I nodded toward the lost souls roaming the hallways.

He fisted his hands until his knuckles whitened and walked past me to cross the threshold. It appeared that he wasn't done with this discussion, but I was.

I slammed the door in his face.

I should have felt empowered for throwing Brandon out, but it only left me with a dull, numbing ache. I marched into the shower in the bathroom and climbed in, turning the water to the highest possible setting.

Whatever closure I had sought, Brandon had given it to me. All remnants of hope that had accidentally lingered were gone. I was numb from both the scalding water and from being railroaded by Brandon over and over.

I hopped out of the shower and threw on a pair of black shorts and a tank top with a built-in bra. The door made a beeping noise, forcing my glance away from the full-length mirror, fingers frozen mid-task of wringing out the tangles from my damp hair.

"Mia," Milo called out, swiping his key card to enter my room. In true older brother fashion, his eyes were downcast in case something unsavory was on display.

I shook my head at his modesty. "Yes, darling brother?"

"Where have you been? You didn't respond to any of my texts."

I unlocked my phone, and sure enough, Milo had sent a few texts in the last half hour.

"I was here." Technically, the truth.

"Then why didn't you answer? I was worried sick that you got kidnapped or something and ended up leaving my meeting early. I can't track your phone here, and you know how much I hate not knowing where you are."

I resisted the urge to roll my eyes.

Milo and Raven drew dramatic conclusions if I didn't respond within five freaking minutes. The only times they backed off was whenever I was left to be supervised by the other.

Using my thumb, I pointed over my shoulder at the bathroom. "Phones aren't conducive during a relaxing bubble bath."

"Bubble bath?" he echoed, seemingly unsatisfied with the explanation.

"Yes." I scowled at my reflection in the mirror, chastising myself for not coming up with a better excuse. How Brandon managed to rattle me so quickly was beyond my comprehension. "I fell asleep in the tub. That's why I didn't respond," I concluded lamely.

"Fell asleep?" Milo strolled closer and laid his palm flat on my forehead. "That could be a sign of fever. There's a virus going around."

I pulled his hand down with a half-smile. "I'm fine."

My heart lurched at his concern. If Milo thought I was sick, he'd probably fly across the globe to bring me soup. He was always doing stuff like that. Took care of me before he was old enough to take care of himself.

Milo was only eight when Mom took a nosedive into Postpartum. Dad worked all the time and simply hired a nanny to fill in the gap Mom had left.

I hated nannies, escalating my attachment to Milo. From what I heard, it started with small acts like changing my diapers and feeding me. Soon, I didn't want to be separated from him, and he never forced me even though it cost him his own childhood.

Milo always put me first. Parents were supposed to do that, not brothers. He didn't ask for this, it wasn't his responsibility, yet he never complained.

Even on days he was too exhausted, Milo never failed to help me with my homework or read me a book at bedtime. We were rich now, but when we were growing up, there had been struggles with money to keep up the façade of a lifestyle Dad had built. Yet,

Milo shielded me from it all and never left me wanting for anything.

Fuck. I am the shittiest person on this earth.

There was only one person I could have fucked to hurt Milo, and I did it. It wasn't only because they had been friends their entire lives or because Brandon watched me grow up. Milo also lacked a certain respect for Brandon.

Milo was the golden boy—responsible, courteous, admirable. Never did drugs, hated tattoos, stayed within the lines, didn't even so much as indulge in an unconventional haircut. He was the kind of man who stopped to help old ladies cross the street.

Brandon was the polar opposite—brooding, tatted-up bad boy—who honked if old ladies didn't move their asses fast enough.

They were oil and water. If they didn't grow up together, I very much doubted they'd be friends today.

I resumed brushing my hair, but my hands shook uncontrollably. My shoulders tensed when Milo noticed it as well.

I can't do this.

I couldn't keep my emotions in check for two more days with Brandon in the same hotel, a walking reminder of what I had done. I felt sullen and disappointed in myself, and the last person I could face right now was my hero.

When I glanced back at his reflection, I found Milo marching toward the adjoining door of our two rooms. He was busy fiddling with his phone. Milo forgot to open the door leading to his room in his absentmindedness, his hand hovering over the knob as he finished typing out an email.

"Milo..." I hesitated.

"Hmm?" he asked, eyes still on his phone.

"I was thinking of returning to Paris tomorrow morning."

Milo's demeanor shifted. Just the slightest alteration in body language, the way his knuckles were whitening against the door handle, and the way his shoulders tensed.

"I thought you were spending a few more days with me. I'm traveling non-stop after this trip and won't see you for a few months."

It wasn't a rebuttal but a statement to outline his unspoken thoughts. I asked to return to Paris, but all he heard was that I'd rather spend my vacation with Raven.

Milo and Raven had an awful falling out before she moved to Paris. They didn't even want to be in the same room anymore.

As a result, my life had mimicked that of a child of divorce. It was a weird analogy, but the only suitable one. Their separation was an ugly divorce with alternating holidays and pressure to take sides.

My birthday had become a point of discord. Every year, I found myself praying they'd simply forget. No such luck.

One year, Raven offered to fly me out to Paris. Milo also planned something for the same weekend. Since he worked all the time, I agreed to go with Milo's plans, rescheduling with Raven for the following weekend. Raven gave me no grief with a "whatever you want" smile. Later, I found out she'd spent a lot of money to take Gabby and me on a surprise weekend cruise.

I felt like the worse scum on earth.

Holidays were worse. I spent part of my winter break in New York and the rest in Paris. This year was no different, except Milo invited me to Nice for New Year's while Raven and Reid opted for a trip to Barcelona. If I had gone with them, Milo would have spent his New Year's Eve working, having gotten into the habit of pushing his friends away.

No matter what I chose, I was letting one of them down. And cutting this trip short only made it seem like I was picking Raven over him. It was furthest from the truth. Milo was my favorite person in the world.

"I'm sorry," I said softly. "I didn't realize how many assignments I still had to finish over winter break."

"You can do them here."

"I forgot my books and... I'm getting really stressed out about the workload. It'll be better if I return to Paris."

He gazed, bleary-eyed. "I got us tickets to a comedy show tomorrow."

"You don't speak French."

"It's a British comedian." When I didn't respond, he followed up with, "They also serve dinner. It's supposed to be really good." I caught the slight trace of disappointment in his tone.

Unfortunately, I couldn't meet Milo's gaze, feeling incredibly guilty in the expensive room Milo had paid for while Brandon stayed in the same hotel.

"I'm so sorry. I should have planned better," I tried to soften the blow.

The trees rustled outside through the clear window, and it appeared to be a cold, windy night. However, it was colder inside this room.

Milo watched me dispassionately without uttering another word. He wouldn't argue over my need for academic excellence, but he could also sniff out my bullshit like a bloodhound.

"Okay," he replied at long last as he shut the door behind him. There was no emotion behind the word, yet it spoke volume.

With two hands on my face, I sagged against the tall mirror, body depleted from exhaustion and mind fucked beyond all rationale.

Mia

THE SUN WAS BARELY above the horizon when Milo dropped me off at the airport. I booked the earliest possible flight out of Nice, leaving me with a measly two hours to sleep.

Milo didn't utter a single word as we hugged goodbye, and when I offered to visit him at his next destination, he reminded me of his busy schedule. My abrupt departure had stunk up the air that was now dripping with resentment. No matter how much I tried to reassure him this was about school, Milo was convinced I had chosen Raven over him—the ultimate slap on his face.

Milo needed time to lick his wounds. While I understood, my spirits lagged during the walk to the terminal gate. My morning was completed as I boarded and broke a nail while stuffing my carry-on suitcase into the overhead compartment.

"Perfect," I scoffed before ducking under the open overhead bin and buckling into my seat.

God, I detested flying alone. To be honest, I hated doing anything by myself, which was a paradox for the otherwise lonely life I led. I preferred company, listening to others speak, hearing their ideas. I particularly loved the companionship of those who took care of me.

It wasn't the most admirable quality in a "strong, independent woman," but relying on others had been hardwired into my personality.

The times I tried to harness more independence didn't amount to much. At some point, I got comfortable with the notion of someone else taking care of things at my behest. For the longest time, it was Milo. After graduating college, he bought a condo and became extremely busy with work. Though he stayed with us every time he returned to New York, his extended business trips ensured his visits were few and far between.

Since Milo didn't trust our parents, a barrage of nannies and babysitters came over in his absence. It was humiliating to have a nanny at my age. Milo knew how much I despised this arrangement and always had them arrive under an abundance of false pretenses such as, *"We are here to help out with your mom."*

Whenever high school was out of session, I flew out to Paris. Raven was even more protective than Milo. When I texted her last night with my flight details, she insisted on picking me up. Raven wouldn't allow me to take a cab or train, though it'd take her over an hour to get to the airport.

Ironically, the flight itself was shorter than her commute to the airport. We landed within thirty minutes. I disembarked with the remaining passengers, pasting on a big, bright smile. Raven was already wary of my abrupt departure from Nice. I needed to get my shit together before she suspected there was more to the story.

I located Raven as soon as the double doors swung open. She was waiting with an iced coffee in hand, along with some sort of sandwich.

She threw up an enthusiastic wave, smiling brighter than the sun itself. As it often happened, I felt awestruck by her beauty at first glance. Her hair was up in sleek do, makeup perfectly polished. Ever the fashion designer, Raven was dressed in a chic outfit—leggings, gray sweater, oversized scarf, and a black coat tied around the waist. Few men turned their heads to check her out, though her beaming face was unaware.

"Hey, babe." Raven threw one arm around my neck. "How was your flight?"

"Good." Standing my carry-on next to me, I hugged her back tightly, cherishing the warmth.

Melting into Raven's kindness was exactly what I needed. After Italy, it took me months to put the pieces back together. One encounter with Brandon and my recently mended heart was shattered into a million pieces. If possible, it hurt more this time because Brandon crushed any spec of hope I had stashed away.

"You okay?" Raven pulled back to shove the iced drink and breakfast sandwich into my open hands.

"Just tired," I mumbled.

"Aww, obviously. It was an early fight."

Shit. She probably woke up even earlier to pick me up. This airport pick-up policy made no sense to me. I regularly took cabs in New York and Paris, so what difference did it make if I took one from the airport.

"Rave... Thanks for waking up so early to pick me up. But you should've just let me take a taxi home."

"What!? No way. What if someone kidnaps you?"

Dear God.

This overprotective nature took a toll on my siblings. They were in their twenties, the peak of their lives. Instead of living it fully, they were busy worrying about me, which only solidified the inconvenience I caused.

A vision of my trip with Brandon flashed in my mind. In the short time that I had spent with him, I never felt like an imposition or a chore. Brandon acted like being needed was a privilege. Perhaps we were a better fit than I cared to admit.

I shook the thought away immediately.

No! Absolutely not. I'm not going there again. I hate him. I hate him.

How much heartbreak did a girl need to endure before it was drilled into her brain that Brandon Cooper was bad news? Time and time again, he proved how wrong I had been about him all these years. He was such a dick and reacted exactly the way I had feared he would if he found out the truth.

"Other people take cabs from the airport." I absentmindedly followed Raven as she grabbed my carry-on suitcase.

"Yes, but young American girls at an airport are prime targets for predators. Haven't you seen the movie *Taken*? Two-seventeen-year-olds were kidnapped in Paris after taking a taxi from the airport."

Instead of pointing out that Raven was also seventeen when she moved to Paris, I focused on my first hit of coffee. I was drained from my battle with Brandon and the earlier brush-off from Milo. The last thing I wanted was to argue with one more person I loved. Today, I only wanted to hear comforting words.

Raven ushered me outside and toward the parking lot. A gust of cold air hit my face. Unlike Nice, Paris was a few degrees colder, which meant that in 3... 2... 1... "Mia, put on your jacket, please," there'd be a comment about my attire.

The predictability made me smile. My jacket dangled through the loop of my arms. I shrugged it on compliantly but paused midway when I spotted the car Raven had led me to. There was nothing remarkable to report other than a red car with four doors. It was the familiar figure leaning against the trunk that had caught my attention.

"Morning!"

Thoughts of Brandon and Milo disappeared entirely. I shrieked from excitement as Reid wrapped an arm around me and lifted me off the ground. The last thing I expected was to see was another Sinclair face in Paris.

Unlike my relationship with Raven and Milo, Reid was less of a parental figure. He was protective but only the appropriate amount for an older brother.

Reid set me down and untangled himself. Much like Raven, he was dressed well—blue jeans, black peacoat with a white shirt underneath—which undoubtedly cost a fortune.

However, it was apparent that the sight of me wasn't as equally pleasant.

"You look like shit. Was the flight that bad?"

Squinting at my reflection on the car window, I couldn't help but agree. I didn't sleep much and chose to forgo my makeup routine in the morning.

Milo, Reid, and Raven always dressed well in public despite the hour or occasion. Keeping with the big city appeal, they were sticklers for presentation. It was one of the reasons why I felt compelled to elevate my own looks. It's also why I had become efficient at makeup and had come to love it.

But on days I chose to skip the routine—like today—I wondered how my average traits compared.

Men openly ogled my beautiful sister. Girls walking past us did a double-take of my handsome brother as well. When we were younger, their entire group of friends walked around like they were the kings and queens of New York. They had what everyone else desired—good looks, money, popularity.

I was starkly different from the rest of my tribe. Stragglers frowned when they saw the oddball out riding the coattails of their attractive counterparts.

"I didn't get a lot of sleep," I lamented.

"Here, I got it." Reid grabbed the suitcase from Raven and opened the trunk. "That's what you get for booking a flight at ass-o-clock in the morning. Do you know what time we had to wake up?"

"But I told Raven *not* to pick me up," I argued. "I could have taken a cab."

"So, you get kidnapped, and Milo blames us for not picking you up? No, thank you."

I rolled my eyes so hard they were probably in the back of my head. "Who are all these people trying to kidnap me?"

"Just watch that movie. What's it called?" Reid snapped his fingers, trying to recall the title. "It had Liam Neeson in it."

I closed my eyes. "Taken," I replied ruefully.

"Yup. That's it."

Instead of festering on the stale topic, I redirected Reid's attention. "What are you doing in Paris?" Raven and Reid went to Spain for New Year's Eve with their group of friends. I assumed he'd return to New York right after.

Reid threw the suitcase in the trunk. "I came to help Raven move."

I leaned back. "Help Raven move?" *We're moving?* I glanced at Raven.

When she first moved to Paris, Raven moved around a lot, unable to settle on an apartment, which meant that I was shuffled from place to place.

Every summer, I spent three months in Paris. I also spent three weeks of winter vacation here, along with spring break and every long weekend.

Last year, I had 165 school days. Out of the remaining 200 days when I was off from school, I spent 174 of it in France. I went to school in New York yet spent half my year in Paris.

Didn't I at least deserve a heads up if my residence for half the year was to change?

"Rave, what's he talking about?" I tried again, but my inquisition was trumped by the loud, jarring noise of Reid slamming the trunk shut.

"Rave, can you hand me the parking stub?"

Raven frowned. "The, what?"

"Parking stub. I slipped it in your purse when we entered the lot."

"Umm... okay." Raven fussed over her purse.

"What does it look like?"

"It's white with a bar code on it."

My mind was still reeling from Reid's comment. I had told Raven multiple times how much I loathed our previously unstable living situation. Raven wouldn't move again without discussing it with me first. Right? I desperately needed an answer.

"Rave, are we moving?" I asked her with more urgency this time.

"One sec, babe," Raven dismissed me absentmindedly. "Reid, I don't see any parking stub. Are you sure it's in my purse?"

"Positive."

I waved my hand to get Raven's attention. "Rave—"

"Not now, Mia," Reid cut me off callously, moving closer to presumably help Raven search. "Check the inner pocket."

I had phrased a question that should take mere seconds to answer. Perhaps they were distracted by the parking slip debacle, but deep down, I knew better.

One-on-one, all of my siblings could hold a conversation with me. However, they actively tuned me out in group settings. Within five minutes of an airport pick-up, I had lost their attention.

Generally speaking, I had gotten used to being ignored. However, the simple answer they were withholding could impact one of the last remaining positives in my life.

Over the years, our house in New York had truly morphed into a ghost town. Our parents might have moved back from Grand Cayman, but Mom still stayed locked in her room. I had no relationship with Dad. Reid moved out years ago for college, and Milo constantly traveled for work.

My only companions were the beloved string of nannies.

It was my lonesome self versus a big empty haunted house. It's the reason I cherished smaller spaces, like our apartment in Paris. I felt more at home in that tiny apartment than inside our mansion on the Upper West Side.

While long flights and jetlag had become second nature—and being shuffled back and forth between the two cities caused instability—it was all worth it when we found a permanent address in Paris. A two-bedroom apartment in an eclectic neighborhood, where eccentric personalities weren't as easily rejected because they were a dime a dozen.

Raven and I loved the apartment. I even felt optimistic enough to decorate my room this time. Not to mention, Gabby and her family lived in the same building. She was the only one who knew what happened with Brandon and had been there for me through thick and thin. If I texted her in the middle of the night, she'd come rushing over.

During my time in Paris, we regularly had visitors, keeping our place loud and vibrant. It was the only place where I wasn't alone.

And now... I was being uprooted yet again without so much as an acknowledgment of the fact.

It sucked.

A five-year-old was informed when their parents planned to move. I was less significant than a child. I was more like the family dog they strutted around, set boundaries for, and then placed wherever they pleased.

I blinked away the tears and pressed for answers. "Please just say yes or no." I heard the hysteria in the way my voice went up an octave.

Raven's brows were pressed together as she concentrated on the contents of the purse. "Reid, it's not in here," she announced.

Reid opened the purse wider to help her dig through the satchel. "It has to be."

Damnit, stop ignoring me.

Neither of them was aware of how much I needed this comfort today. I couldn't recoup what happened with Brandon, Milo was giving me the silent treatment, and there was nothing left for me in New York. The only thing I had looked forward to was face-planting on my bed, crying for hours, and talking to Gabby.

Instead, my last semblance of stability was being taken away. I could understand if there were logical reasons, but I wasn't provided with any. I was barely informed then promptly ignored, like always. They'd rather bicker about a ticket than take two seconds out of their lives to answer a simple *yes* or *no* question.

"Maybe it's lost," Raven announced. "Whatever. Let's just pay the maximum price for the day and get the hell out of here."

"We can't," Reid argued. "It's cash only. When was the last time any of us carried cash?"

"Fuck!"

"I know," he droned. "Ugh! This sucks. I need to go back to sleep. I'm still hungover as shit."

"Let's check the car. Maybe it fell when you tried to slip it in my purse."

"At least tell me if we are moving to a new neighborhood." I might as well have spoken into the air.

Raven and Reid rounded each side and threw the doors open to check every crevice inside the car. I remained rooted in place, somewhere between flabbergasted and mentally drained.

I sighed, staring ahead blankly. "I'm considering getting a new part-time job. Given my sporadic love for public nudity, I believe exotic dancing to be the most fitting. Now, I know what you're thinking. The shifts are a real bitch but don't worry. I'll always be home by curfew on school nights." I nodded sharply with vindication.

"Do you see anything?"

"No. Check the glove compartment."

"But that doesn't mean we have to close other avenues of opportunities. One of my friends recently joined this organization called MS-13. Other than getting a few face tattoos to mark something called a kill list, he said the training process was a breeze." I waved it off.

"I see something sticking out from under the mat."

"Found it." Reid held up a slip.

"Pluuuuus, no taxes. Cha-ching. Mia for the win."

"Oh, thank god." Raven turned to me. "Mia, did you just say something?"

I stared at Raven impassively.

Reid quirked an eyebrow over my extended silence. "Don't just stand there quietly. It's rude not to answer when someone asks you a question."

And that broke the camel's back.

Before I could stop myself, I chucked the empty drink against the concrete, screamed that they were both out of their fucking minds, and stormed off.

No longer could I ignore the acceleration in my pulse. Erratic emotions rose even as I reminded myself to calm down.

It had been years since I'd had a meltdown. I practiced meditation, redirected my attention to different things the way Milo had taught me, kept myself occupied. Apparently, fragments of my behavior couldn't be expelled during a heartbreak.

"What the fuck, Mia?" I heard Reid's shouting while Raven called out hysterically.

I used to regret my meltdowns after the fact, but I lacked the ability to make the distinction in the spur of the moment. I found myself standing in front of a cab. It was a reflexive action out of sheer spite. Grabbing the handle, I pulled the backseat door wide open and rattled off an address.

Guilt hit me when I saw Reid and Raven's perplexed faces from a distance. I considered pulling the taxi over, but the thought of being ignored for the next hour while stuck in a small car kept me seated.

Fuck it! I'd rather get kidnapped.

* * *

"I heard you're in trouble," Gabby whispered. I moaned, pulling the comforter over my face to drown out her voice. Gabby and I were supposed to hang out later in the day. Why was she here so early? I was nowhere ready to wake up.

Reid and Raven called me relentlessly during my taxi ride home. They eventually gave up, texting we'd meet at home to talk about what happened.

Having arrived before them, I had instinctively searched for my book. When I remembered the sequence of events, I leaned against the bed frame, closed my eyes, and listened to the sounds filtering through the balcony. I wanted to cry my heart out until I was tapped dry. Instead, I crawled under the comforter. I had already wasted enough tears on that stupid story.

When my bedroom door creaked open, I pretended to be asleep upon hearing Raven's subsequent sigh from under the comforter. She let me be, but I knew a lecture was waiting for me.

I peeked through the comforter to glance at the clock. It was almost three p.m., even though it felt like only minutes had passed.

"Raven let you in?" I groggily mumbled.

"Mm-mmm." Gabby stretched out next to me, her head hitting the same pillow as mine.

Pulling the comforter down, I turned to face her.

"Did she tell you what happened?" I asked nervously.

"Only that you stormed off at the airport. And to make it a short visit because Raven wants to talk to you when you wake up." Gabby closed her eyes, looking ready for a nap herself.

"Did she tell you why I stormed off?" I pressed.

"Nope. Said it was totally out of the blue." Gabby opened one eyelid. "She asked if it was boy-related."

I bit the insides of my cheeks. Every time I expressed one single emotion, Raven assumed it was the aftereffect of a boy who ruined me. Her theory was spot on during this specific situation, but that was beside the point.

Reid and Raven had no clue how they behaved around me. Whenever I brought it to their attention, they either dismissed it or promised to do better, neither of which yielded positive changes.

"What did you tell her?"

"The truth," Gabby said plainly. "You did the nasty with Brandon, and this behavior was part of the moping around since the fuck-fest. Should have seen the way Raven turned red. You Americans are such prudes."

"You're an American," I pointed out.

"Barely," she countered. "I moved here when I was eight. At this point, I have lived in France most of my life. The stature of limitation has expired."

"Uh-huh." I yawned. "So, what did you actually tell Raven?"

Gabby sighed, turning to lie on her side. "That you were the purest virgin to grace this earth. And if you were ever to get pregnant, it'd be nothing short of miraculous inception."

"Immaculate conception," I corrected. "You're forgetting all of your English," I tutted.

"Yes, that," Gabby dismissed. "Told her that I had planned to buy you a cast-iron chastity belt for your birthday, but all of the customer satisfaction reviews were terrible."

"Hilarious."

Gabby shrugged. "I thought so, but Raven didn't find it funny." She tucked her hands under her face, her beautiful dark hair spilling to the side. She scrutinized me quietly before opening her mouth again. "Mia... does any of this have to do with Brandon?"

"No," I replied without hesitation.

Brandon played a huge role in what happened today. I was used to being ignored and taught myself to be okay with it, but the run-in with him left me shaken. I was seeking a bit of comfort, not the usual dismissal.

But I didn't have the heart to tell Gabby that. She was the only one who knew about him (minus his age) and liked to romanticize the fling—being whisked away and all that. Every time she did, it gave me false hope.

Brandon had given me the necessary wake-up call. I had to eradicate all hopes and dreams, focusing only on the reality of the situation. While my positive outlook was shattered, I didn't have to destroy Gabby's.

"Hmm," she silently challenged my proclamation, her bright hazel eyes taunting me. "I have never known you to get into trouble. But since this Brandon dude, it seems like you can't stay out of it."

I groaned again, sitting up.

Before I could voice a convincing response, my bedroom door flew open. The formidable jury was here to hand out the verdict.

"Hey, you're up," Raven said cautiously, approaching me as if I was about to go off the handle again. Reid wasn't far behind. He didn't say anything, though shades of disapproval were written all over his face.

"I was just leaving." Gabby sat up, reading the tension in the room. "Call me later." She blew me a kiss and practically ran for the door.

Judas.

Reid waited to hear the front door shut before turning to me. "What the hell, Mia?" he snapped. Raven patted Reid's arm with an unspoken signal.

Of the duo, Raven was the reasonable one. On the other hand, Reid displayed all the classic symptoms of a middle child. Whereas my meltdowns were impulsive, Reid's hot-headedness was routine. He'd likely come down on me the hardest for today's antics.

"How are you feeling?" Raven asked me nervously.

"We were worried sick," Reid charged ahead. "What if something had happened to you?"

"From taking a cab?" I couldn't help but retort. "I'm seventeen. Both of you traveled alone at my age."

"That's because we had common sense. We were independent and aware of our surroundings. You might be a brainiac, but you have zero concept of how the real world works."

I hated when they threw those words in my face. How did they expect me to learn when they wouldn't allow me to do one thing by myself?

It was a Catch 22.

"Okay. Everyone take a deep breath." Raven pressed her palm on Reid's chest and pushed him back.

I preemptively declared, "I'm sorry."

Reid was right.

I could speak like an adult, provide advice, discuss politics and religion. But there was no real-world application for my knowledge. I had no idea how to navigate life as an adult. My embarrassing actions today were only indicative of the fact. I lacked impulse control and desperately wished I had done things differently.

"It's ok—" Raven started, but Reid cut her off.

"The worst part is that we don't even know what sparked it."

I was numb from fighting. "I kept asking you guys over and over again if we were moving. You kept dismissing me. You always do that," I added in a small voice.

Raven and Reid exchanged a look. Since they were babies, those two could basically read each other's minds. I was pretty sure they had a language of their own. I couldn't always crack the code, but this one was easy.

They were gearing up to reveal something big.

"What's going on?" I asked.

They both sat on either edge of my bed. "Mia," Raven started. "I have some news."

"It's good news," Reid added. "So, I want you to be happy for Raven."

I stared at him. It only meant Raven was moving to a place I'd hate.

"Raven's moving back to New York."

I was right.

"Are you all right?" Raven asked without missing a beat.

I sat up on the bed and crossed my legs. "When?"

They exchanged another look. "Immediately. I came to help her move."

I looked down at my hands. If Raven wasn't in Paris anyone, it meant that I had no reason to visit. Everything I built here, the friendships, all gone. Poof.

"It's going to be okay," she said quietly.

I smiled sadly, determined not to have a repeat of the earlier showdown. Raven scooted closer and wrapped an arm around me to pull me closer. It was the comfort I had longed for all day.

"Why don't I order some lunch? You must be starving."

I meekly nodded as she smoothed a hand down my hair.

Raven kissed my temple. It was something all three of them practiced whenever they wanted to console me. Mom never tucked me in or kissed me goodnight. So, they always did it on her behalf. I suspected that the habit had remained with them even after all these years.

Raven sprung to her feet and whispered, "It'll be great. I promise." She left the room to find our stack of take-out menus.

I stared out the window, which overlooked the busy street. "Do you know why she is moving?"

"Mia... Raven is..." Reid shifted uncomfortably. "She's moving because she has no other choice. Raven's mom lost her business."

My head whipped back. "Wait, what?"

"It just happened. They are shutting down the boutique. Raven thought it was time to move back and be near her real family. The two of us."

My breath caught. Raven was broke? All this time, she had been paying for my flights to Paris and everything else. Fuck. I was such an insensitive jerk to her.

"I can't believe it."

"I know," he sighed.

"Will she be okay? I have that emergency fund from Milo—"

Reid smiled, patting the top of my head. "She won't take Milo's money. You know that. I offered, too."

"So, what then?"

"We just have to be supportive."

I nodded.

It made sense for Raven to be near us during her time of need. After our family fostered her, she became closer to us than her own. Our parents were negligent at best, but Raven's parents straight up abandoned her. She moved to Paris to develop a better relationship with them, but it never panned out.

Reid nudged me, returning to the previous topic. "So, apparently, we ignore you."

"All the damn time," I replied sulkily.

"I think you might be right."

It was a dynamic I had taught myself to accept, especially in groups. Then Brandon saw me when I never expected him to notice. I hated the asshole but did learn a lesson in the midst. Captivating someone's attention had changed how okay I was with this arrangement.

I craved to be seen. I yearned to be heard.

"It's normal for the youngest child to be seen, not heard," Reid said uncertainly as a timid way of explaining.

"It sucks."

"It does. And it isn't fair."

This wasn't the first time they had acknowledged this issue, but it was the first time I felt determined to change the outcome.

Reid eyed me somberly, mouth set into a thin line. "But do you think the best way to change your circumstance is by being so reactive? Running off only proved the opposite of your point."

I stared at my hands. "I really am sorry about today."

He sighed. "You talk and act like a grown-up, which is great. But you're also too trusting, and we worry about how easily someone can take advantage of that, especially with your tendency to make rash decisions. It takes time to gain experience, so just exercise some patience. Okay?"

I nodded.

In Nice, I blindly trusted Brandon and followed him to Italy. It quickly went south, and he almost held me there against my will.

Afterward, I entrusted a total stranger to take me to the ferry. The fisherman who gave me a ride turned out to be nice, but it could have easily gone awry as well, with me locked up in his basement.

Raven would faint if she found out about the first real taste of freedom I had experienced. And Reid would have a heart attack if he found out how I had maneuvered through it.

My naive nature concerned him, and rightfully so because these thoughts never crossed my mind until this very second when he pointed it out.

"Besides, Raven worries about you too much. Right now, we need to be there for her. If she thinks you are regressing, she's going to focus on you instead of concentrating on starting her career as she should."

My compulsions were difficult to suppress, but Reid was right. Raven would worry more if she thought my worst habits were returning.

I pursed my lips. "I'll try to be better."

"Mia, I know it's difficult for you because you express things the way you see them—plainly. But it doesn't hurt to apply tact or think things through. If you can do that, I promise we'll listen to what you want as well."

He inclined his head.

"And if that includes becoming a stripper or joining MS-13, then so be it." His eyes danced with amusement.

I bit back a smile. "The struggle is real out there."

Reid was giving me a compromise along with a motivation. A behavior I had to eradicate from my life in exchange for something I desperately wanted.

"So, all three of us are going back together?"

"Yup. Are you going to be okay?"

I swallowed hard. "I'll miss Gabby, but I'll be fine."

Reid kissed my forehead, and just like Raven, he also whispered, "It'll be great," before leaving.

And just like with Raven, I didn't believe him either.

Mia

The day started as had many, blurring with the rest. I sat on my windowsill, uncaring about the chilliness dragged through the open window.

Lifting my hand, I shielded my eyes from direct contact with the sunrays and stared at my neighborhood. The red and gray brownstones glistened in the morning sun. On Sundays, there was barely any foot traffic on our street.

It had been days since our return to New York. The last flight leaving Paris in the rearview mirror felt like the end of an era. It was only six and a half hours travel time to New York, but the two cities couldn't be more different. And the view of the Upper West Side didn't quite compare to the view of Paris from my old room.

The architecture in Paris was more unique. Life was more exciting. People were more interesting. No matter what, Paris still felt like home, and a small part of my heart would always remain there.

Life in New York had promptly resumed to normal. It was my senior year with college on the horizon. I should be working on my college applications but hadn't found the motivation. Instead, I was preoccupied.

Though he played it off, Milo was hurt by my early departure from Nice. My brother was a busy man and had cleared his schedule with the expectation that we'd spend time together.

Meanwhile, I couldn't bear to face Brandon. But leaving so hastily was inconsiderate since Milo went through the trouble of planning a mini-vacation for us.

My impulsiveness had overruled the best of my intentions yet again, making me appear ungrateful for the privileged life he provided.

Neither of us discussed my faux pas again, and I had been careful not to even mention Raven's name. Things were still painfully awkward during our phone calls. From his line of comments, it was clear Milo was available if I needed anything. Otherwise, senseless chit-chat had become like pulling teeth. After a few phone calls of similar nature, I took the hint and left him alone.

There was a growing rift between us, and I had no idea how to fix it. I kept waiting for things to revert to normal and could hardly concentrate until they did.

Nonetheless, an onslaught of nannies still dropped by every evening, no doubt to report my progress to Milo. I did my best not to cause any trouble, hoping the positive feedback would improve our relationship.

So far, it hadn't.

I glanced at my phone to find a message from Raven, asking if I had eaten breakfast. I took a photo of the yogurt I had been picking at and sent it to her.

The excitement of having Raven back was also starting to wear thin. Raven was full of warmth and always had a loving effect on our home. I had hoped we'd find the same vibrancy once she moved back. Perhaps do more sisterly things together. When we lived in Paris, we stayed up, watched movies, talked into the night. But Raven had been swamped with work, leaving me with my lonely thoughts. Lots of lonely nights, too, that had me missing the furnace to once wrap me in his warmth.

Brandon had roused something uncontrollable inside me. The naïve side of me never considered sexual revolution a rite of passage until I crossed that threshold. It was impossible to deny that life was lackluster without the burning passion Brandon had introduced.

Fucking Brandon.

It was such a precarious situation that I could never disclose the whole truth to anyone, even to Gabby.

I dropped my face in between my hands and groaned.

Perhaps, I simply needed to rid the thoughts of these sins. And what better day to do so than on God's day.

When I was young, the only thing I did with Dad was to attend church together on Sundays. In our home, there was a fifty-fifty split on religion. Reid and I were avid believers, whereas Raven and Milo were atheists.

Milo struggled to understand how someone like me, who loved science, believed in a higher power. In my opinion, optimism and realism could peacefully coincide. The same dash of optimism could get me out of this funk.

A spontaneous idea crossed my mind.

My fingers hovered over the lock screen of my phone before typing out a text, asking Raven and Reid to join me for church.

"No way!"

The group thread with Reid and Raven blew up. Not only had they agreed, but they suggested grabbing lunch afterward. With a renewed sense of purpose, I peeled myself off the sill.

Heartbreak had fogged my mind. How I had been acting, it wasn't me. I wasn't a pessimistic person. I needed to return to my roots and look at life through positive lenses.

Teeming with a new spirit, I searched my closet for a church-friendly outfit and, within the hour, left my house in slacks, a sweater, and a puffy jacket.

A beautiful day awaited me outside. It was the day all the hurt and pain would be replaced with purpose. I just needed to redirect my focus to something better.

"Where to?" The cab driver asked, chewing on a toothpick that stuck out.

I spat out the address and leaned back against the seat. There were rips on the seat's fabric, and it was in desperate need of an upgrade. I wasn't bothered. The point of today was to start fresh with an optimistic outlook.

When we arrived, the cab driver peered out of the driver's side window as I dug through my purse for the fare. I could feel his sidelong glance. It was unusual for someone my age to voluntarily attend church alone. Most teenagers were dragged to church by their family members.

"Here you go." I handed him the cash and hopped out.

"Mia. Over here."

Reid and Raven were outside of the church door. Despite the weather, Raven was in a green Sunday dress, the waistband of her coat wrapped tightly around her middle. Even Reid dressed up in slacks and a button-down, which made me happy that they put in the effort. Another positive.

"You guys look nice."

Raven smiled warmly. "Glad you approve. I had no idea what to wear."

Reid sniggered behind Raven. "She googled *appropriate attire for church.*"

I shook my head and laughed.

"Shall we?" Reid held open the door for us.

The church interior was a sight to behold and could transport you back in time. It was decorated in ornate colors with pops of gold and white linings. It was Raven's first time, and I caught her stealthily taking photos of the beautiful surroundings.

The masses had already congregated for service, so we sat in the back row. The wooden bench wasn't the most comfortable, but it could be worse.

"Mia!" Someone grabbed the back of my shoulders and shook me.

Surprised, Reid and Raven jumped, ready to fight off the perpetrator. I turned to find a friendly face staring back.

"Oh my God, Chris." Reaching out, I tugged him into a warm hug. It had been months since I last saw him.

Raven cleared her throat at my unusual display of affection. I dismissed her and ended the hug only when I was good and ready.

God, I had missed Chris, along with everyone else at this church. I had been so busy wallowing that I had pulled back from the community. Chris' smiling face reminded me how much I missed this place and vowed to rectify the situation.

Chris rubbed both of my shoulders in an up and down motion; his handsome face lit up like a starry night. He might as well be the poster child for the all-American good look—blond, blue eyes, tall. No tattoos or messy hair to report, unlike some people I knew. He was clean-shaven and dressed in slacks with a blue button-down shirt and tie.

"It's been so long. Where have you been?"

"Got a little busy with the holidays and my usual visit to Paris... you know." Raven cleared her throat again, this time without exercising any subtlety. Rolling my eyes, I addressed her. "Chris, this is my sister, Raven. And you remember my brother, Reid."

"Hello." Raven gave him a once over.

Reid was friendlier as he had attended church with me before and had seen Chris in passing. "Hey man, how's it going?"

Chris leaned forward. "Good. Glad to see the family's here with

Mia." Then he added in a whisper, so only I'd hear, "And thankfully, no Milo."

I suppressed the laugh that threatened to break free. Milo and Chris had an interesting first meeting. At that time, Chris and I loathed each other. But over the years, we had become good friends.

I beamed at him. "Why don't we catch up? It's been forever."

"Sure. Do you have plans after church?

"Yes," Raven answered on my behalf, not bothering to appear friendly. "We have lunch reservations."

"That's right, we do. And you should come with us," I added without missing a beat, directing a pointed look at Raven.

Reid stared quizzically at Raven, undoubtedly surprised by her unfriendly tone. He hadn't spent months with us in Paris and wasn't used to this side of her.

"Sounds good. I'll find you afterward." Chris waved us goodbye and left to join his family. They sat a few rows behind, dressed in their best Sunday outfits.

"Nice kid," Reid absentmindedly muttered.

"He is," I agreed with Reid, though my eyes were locked on Raven. I never understood why she was so paranoid about men.

Raven didn't utter another word throughout the sermon, but twice I saw her nervous gaze fleet back to Chris. How she could say anything bad about him was beyond me. He was the nicest guy on the planet.

Well, he wasn't always this way. Once upon a time, Chris was even a bully. *My* bully, to be specific.

How the tides had turned.

* * *

"Freak."

I frowned at Chris Allen, who yelled from across the church parking lot. We had only just joined this church, but that guy already had it out for me.

Whatever.

Bullies bored me. They were never shrewd enough for the title, and their insults were uninspired. Freak? It's like he wasn't even trying.

Typically, I'd attend church with Dad, but he was working. It wasn't ideal to attend solo, but at least Milo was nearby. He was doing a group project and dropped me off before meeting with them at a nearby café. While I waited for him to pick me up, I decided to spend the time with some... people watching.

I had once told Brandon that I didn't know how to act normal. Following my admission, I thought he'd give me the same spiel I got from Raven, Reid, and Milo. Something about being yourself to win everyone over.

But as usual, Brandon was the only one to tell me the truth. He had leaned over and whispered, "Fake it till you make it."

It took me a long time to understand his words. I had to mimic others by watching them, at least until the behaviors were ingrained enough for me to become natural at it.

Ignoring Chris' jab, I resumed watching the girls with excellent posture. They also attended church service today and wandered off afterward, searching for a cab.

The early afternoon sun beat down my face. Squinting my eyes, I concentrated against the bright light to make out the two figures in the distance. Both girls were in their early twenties, well put together, and even from here, I could tell they were demure.

I pulled my shoulders back to imitate their postures, speaking to the invisible air around me with the gestures they were making.

"Ow!"

A sharp pain shot through my scalp, making me turn in that direction. A handful of my pigtail was in Chris Allen's burly grip. He tugged on it until I was forced to face him. "I said," he closed in, "freak."

"I heard you." I jerked my hair out of his hold and took a step back. "I have just been called a lot worse by a lot better."

Chris frowned, trying to dissect the insult. His face twisted when he understood it.

"You think you're better than the rest of us?" he asked, voice low as he gained toward me. Despite his respectable church attire, he looked threatening of a white button-down shirt and gray slacks.

My eyes sifted through the empty parking lot. Where were his parents? Most of the congregation seemed to have left as well. Smoothing down the skirt of my yellow dress, I tried to tamper my fear.

I muttered a quick prayer under my breath, hoping Milo could somehow hear it.

"Let me tell you something, freak," Chris continued. "I've seen you stare at everyone at this church like a creep, muttering God knows what to yourself. If you do that one more time, AHHH—"

Chris' was cut off mid-sentence, body levitating. Milo held Chris' shirt collar with one hand, dangling him in thin air. The sun shone behind his head, creating a halo effect. Like a savior, a messiah, Milo was surrounded by the light.

"What are you doing?" Chris yelled. "Put me down."

"Did I just hear you threaten my sister?" Milo asked evenly in the way he did before unleashing hell's fury on someone.

I very much doubted Milo would let Chris go. Not after catching him red-handed in the middle of pushing me around. However, we were in a house of worship. My brother might not believe in it, but I didn't want his eternal soul to burn in hell.

"Milo," I hissed. "What are you doing? Put him down."

"No," Milo replied simply without bothering to spare me a glance. He was staring at Chris, wondering what to do with him. "Kid, where are your parents?"

Chris only struggled harder. A ripping sound emerged from his shirt, no doubt tearing under Milo's grip.

"They went home," Chris snapped. He seemed unapologetic, intent on further inciting Milo's wrath.

I wanted to scream at Chris to shut up. He seemingly thought himself braver, but now wasn't the time to provoke Milo. Not when he was about to hand out Chris' punishment.

"Too bad. I was going to give them a piece of my mind for bad parenting and for letting their freak," Milo emphasized on the word freak, "of a son run around without a leash. Since they aren't here, think I'm going to..." Milo looked around as if searching for inspiration. His eyes zeroed into something nearby. "There. I'm going to hang you off that flagpole and give you some time to reflect on your actions."

Wished I could assent to this being a joke. I had no doubt in my mind that Milo fully planned to carry out this ludicrous sentence. He was a reasonable man until the mama bear side of him took over. Then all bets were off.

"No!" Chris' snarky reserve finally broke, a tinge of fear coming off him. "Please, don't. I'm sorry."

"Milo," I stepped forward with determination. "You need to put that boy down."

Milo finally turned to face me though he made no gesture of letting Chris go. "This little shit thinks he can—"

"Please don't curse in the house of God," I interrupted.

"It's the parking lot, not your precious house of God," he retorted.

I ignored the technicality. "Milo, you really need to put him down before someone sees you."

Chris seemed flabbergasted that his fate was being decided while hanging in mid-air. But he was officially scared of Milo and smartly kept his trap shut.

I tried again. "You're making too big of a deal. Bullying is just a part of life. Some would even say a rite of passage."

Milo huffed. "That's ridiculous. I wasn't bullied."

"Probably because you were the bully."

Milo leaned back, affronted. "I have never bullied anyone in my life."

With my eyes, I pointedly raked the scene in front of me, hinting at the twelve-year-old boy Milo was holding up by the collar.

He rolled his eyes. "It's different. This little shit deserves it."

"I bet that's what he says when he bullies other people," I countered, silently challenging him to disagree.

"Fine. You have a point," he gritted out. It killed him, but Milo always admitted when he had been bested in an argument. "For once, I wished you'd act like a normal eleven-year-old kid."

Chris looked triumphant that his captivity was ending until Milo stampeded all over that hope.

"I'm still not letting this dipshit off the hook." No, I supposed he wouldn't. I expected nothing less. "If I didn't get here in time today—"

"I got lucky that you did," I interrupted. "But next time, you might not get here in time. And if I don't gain the experience to handle myself in these situations, the fallout might be worse."

Milo nodded, considering my words. "I... agree," he said somewhat reluctantly. "What do you propose?"

"Letting me fight my own battles for a change."

Milo stared at the boy he held up in the air. With a sigh, he lowered Chris, though he didn't let go of his grip. "It's your lucky day," he ground out. "Mia needs experience, and apparently, you are an expert in this matter. Go ahead. Bully my sister."

Chris's incredulous face simply shifted back and forth between us, trying to decide if we were a family of loons or if this was a legitimate discussion.

Unfortunately, this was one of our tamer dialects.

Milo raised his brows. "I don't have all day. Start bullying. Mia, do you know how to make a fist?"

Chris was no longer able to process the situation. I felt bad for the guy, but I had only managed to deduce his sentence. If he didn't prove his worth to Milo, he might as well be hanging from that flagpole all night.

"I'm waiting," Milo said impatiently.

I leaned an inch closer and whispered to Chris, "Just pull my hair or something."

Chris' eyes widened for a split second before he jolted out of Milo's grasp and took off at full speed. We stared after him in bewilderment as he managed to skirt past the trash can on the sidewalk and disappear around the corner.

Chapter 18

Mia

THE REMINDER of how my friendship with Chris started only reinforced it was for the best if I put Brandon in the rearview mirror. Personal differences aside, I had no interest in watching him get destroyed by Milo.

Milo shipped off his own mother when her mental health issues threatened my well-being. That's what he did to the woman who gave him life. The man who defiled me never stood a chance. Milo would surely peg Brandon for a sexual predator and go after him with everything. For God's sake, Chris was only a kid, and Milo was still ready to inflict pain on him without remorse.

On the other hand, Chris was grateful for my aide on that fateful day. I had initially thought he was a jackass but was swiftly proven wrong. Chris might be the nicest human being I had ever met.

Throughout the years, the church became our stomping ground. Until six months ago, Chris and I were active members of the church and had worked on plenty of fundraisers together.

When I was fourteen, we even shared a kiss at a church dance. It happened a few more times when I was fifteen. However, it never amounted to anything more between my grueling schedule, Paris, and overprotective siblings.

Our friendship had always been contained to the church grounds, another situation I'd like to rectify. I barely had a social circle in New York, and it'd be nice if that were to change.

By the time church let out, Reid had altered our lunch reservations to add a fourth person. The restaurant was around the corner, so Chris insisted on meeting us there as he still had a few people to greet.

As soon as we were seated at the posh Thai restaurant, I informed our server to wait for the fourth person to put in our orders. However, I wondered if my efforts were in vain as Raven had probably scared Chris off. So, I was pleasantly surprised when he strolled through the front door.

"You guys didn't have to wait for me." He slid into the tufted grey booth, taking the seat next to me.

"Mia made us," Raven mumbled grumpily.

My jaw almost dropped open.

What the actual fuck!?

Since when did Raven make snide comments? She was supposed to be the diplomatic one in our family.

Luckily, Reid came to the rescue. He laughed nervously to diffuse the tension. "Of course, we waited for you." He handed Chris a menu. "Raven's joking."

Chris laughed uncomfortably. "I don't get the joke."

"That's because she didn't tell it right," I chimed in. "What do you think of the Pad Thai?"

Chris stared blankly between us, but being a nice guy, he let it go. "Looks good."

"So, Chris, do you go to school with Mia?" Raven asked as Reid raised his hand to catch the waiter's attention.

"No. But we're in the same grade."

“Oh. So, you’re a year older than her?” When I started senior year, I was only sixteen. As usual, I was the youngest in my class.

"Umm, I guess."

Raven tapped her menu. “Mia is the youngest in her class because her teachers suggested skipping a grade. She was too advanced. IQ of 155.”

IQ of 151, I corrected in my head.

Raven was being deliberately generous about my intellect. A not-so-subtle hint that I was young and sexually inexperienced but too smart to succumb to pressure in case Chris had ulterior motives.

Chris merely smiled. “I believe it.”

The chipper waiter interrupted before Raven could speak again. “Hi folks, how are we doing today?”

While he took our order, Reid glanced at Raven sternly, silently communicating with her. Secret language or not, this time, I understood their exchange. No translation needed.

“Leave him alone.”

“What? I’m just taking an interest in the guy.”

“Well, cut it out. He is a nice kid.”

“Too nice. I don’t buy it.”

As soon as the waiter disappeared, Raven resumed the interrogation. “Chris, I don’t think I caught your last name.”

“It’s Allen.”

Raven furrowed her brows, trying to place the name Allen in our social circle, going through her mental catalog of our contacts. Raven took a diplomatic approach when the name didn't ring a bell. “Does your family know ours by any chance?”

“Maybe through church.” He shrugged with a smile.

Most of the families that attended our church lived on the Upper West Side. We didn’t know all of them, but most were part of similar statuses and social cliques, so she would have at least heard the last name in passing.

Raven frowned, lost in thought.

Aware of her dilemma—refusal to voice an impolite demand of his identity but also unwilling to let me be acquainted with a boy she knew nothing about—Chris bit the bullet and put Raven out of her misery.

"But I highly doubt anyone from your family hangs out with mine."

"How come?"

"Because we live in Harlem, and I don't think the friendship would be very convenient," he pointedly replied. "You know, because of the distance between Harlem and Upper West Side."

Unlike myself, Chris came from humble beginnings. He was attending college in the fall through merit and scholarship, not by paying hefty tuition fees.

Reid coughed uncomfortably at Chris' insinuation of his blue-collar life and modest neighborhood to paint the stark differences in our social standings. I was pretty sure Reid was kicking Raven under the table. She said nothing while I wanted to die of mortification.

Undeterred, Chris charged forward. "It's a long hike, but our family has always attended this church. Guess we are suckers for loyalty."

The waiter returned with our food and set down a curry dish in front of Raven and a Pad Thai for me.

"Thank you." I quietly churned my noodle around my fork, wondering if this lunch was salvageable. Sulkily, I muttered, "Why don't you tell him about my IQ again? That was going really well."

The clinking of forks stopped around the table. Wearily, I glanced up. Reid smirked into his food, attempting to smother a laugh. Raven was biting her lips, embarrassed. However, Chris couldn't hold back.

Laughter bubbled out of his lips, and he threw his head back. It cracked Raven and Reid's restraints as well. The tension diffused under a round of chuckles.

God, Chris could turn any situation around. Everything about him screamed an upstanding member of society. No one was immune to his charms.

As it turned out, not even Raven. "That's wonderful to hear, Chris," Raven said, digging into her Massaman curry. "Sorry for being so intrusive. It's just... very few men seem to have good intentions nowadays."

"No worries." Chris smiled before sweeping the uncomfortable conversation entirely under the rug. "So, do you think you'll join our church?"

Raven laughed. "I don't think I'm your target clientele. But if Mia wants, I can come back next week."

Just like that, Raven's barrage of interrogation concluded, and I found myself unwinding. Apparently, it was Chris' lack of entitlement that soothed her nerves.

Chris wasn't a privileged asshole. Nothing had been handed to him, and men like him worked for their keep. He was as harmless as they came, which Raven loved. It meant that he wouldn't feel entitled to a woman's body if she were to turn him down... unlike this tatted bastard I once knew.

For only the tiniest second, I let my mind wander. Would Raven have given in so easily if Brandon were sitting next to me?

No. She would have stared him down coolly for his entitled attitude and self-absorbed ways.

And Brandon wouldn't have made one single effort to turn the situation around. He wouldn't cater to my family or put their minds at ease. If they didn't like him, he'd blow off their concerns and tell them to go fuck themselves.

But not Chris.

Throughout the rest of lunch, Chris chipped away at Raven's remaining defenses. By the time our waiter brought the bill, they were following each other on Instagram. Practically the best of friends.

Reid snagged the check. "Lunch is on me."

"No way. Let me," Chris protested.

"Nope, we invited you," Reid said decisively and handed his card to the waitress.

It was a relief because I knew Chris was saving up for his remaining college expenses.

Reid stretched his arms over his head. "God, I'm tired." Translation: *I'm still hungover from last night.*

It wouldn't be a Sunday if Reid weren't hungover. I often feared that he might be developing a drinking problem, but when I had brought up the topic to him, I was only met with his wrath.

"Think I'm going to head back," he declared.

"Me too." Raven looked between us, then did something to shock the hell out of me. "But you two should hang out. It's such a nice day outside." She slid a twenty-dollar bill across the table. "Go get some hot chocolate. On me."

Did Raven just encourage me to hang out with a boy... unsupervised?

"Yeah, don't let us old folks hold you back," Reid added.

"I'm down," Chris said easily.

"I guess." I shrugged, staring between the two of them, hardly believing it possible. I had wanted them to give me more independence, and perhaps they were finally doing it.

With quick hugs outside of the restaurant, we exchanged goodbyes. Chris wasn't put off by my siblings setting us up on a mini date. Instead, he dragged me to Central Park to try all the different types of street food.

Chris was affectionate throughout, randomly grabbing my hand without a second thought. He put an arm around my shoulders as he led me down a path. Anyone walking by might presume we were young lovers.

"Hope you're hungry. These are the best crepes in Manhattan."

I laughed. "We just had lunch."

"Then consider it dessert."

"I don't—"

"And here we have a lady with the best roasted pecans in the world."

"The best?"

"Yup. She wrote it down on a sign and everything. So, it must be true."

I laughed again as he pulled me in a million directions, making sure there was never a dull moment.

Hours went by as a realization dawned on me. It was the longest I had gone in my life without thinking about Brandon.

So, when Chris walked me home and leaned in, I didn't deny him. It somehow seemed poetic since he was the first boy I had kissed, though it never quite curled my toes. Then or now.

However, this kiss was more significant than my first. For when I pulled back, one thing was decided on my behalf—I was cured.

My obsession with Brandon Cooper was finally over.

Mia

By the time my last class ended, I practically leaped outside with my phone in hand. Wellington Prep had strict rules about cell phone usage on school grounds. Most kids broke the stipulation. I never did but had a gut feeling that good news was waiting for me.

I turned on my phone on the walk home, anticipating a message or voicemail. Crushing disappointment engulfed me when I saw neither.

Last night, I texted Milo and had hoped he'd respond to the kindly fashioned words. It'd been weeks since Nice, and things were still tense. The strain had left a punctured hole in my chest.

At least, I had a wonderful new boyfriend to focus on instead of wallowing. While the relationship had its challenges, on the account that my boyfriend had no romantic interest in me, I was grateful for Chris.

People said you needed love to survive. I disagreed. Oxygen was a little more important, wouldn't you agree? Love was a mixture of biochemicals—dopamine, oxytocin, vasopressin. Those elements could be manipulated and redirected toward another source if necessary.

Any source, such as Chris.

Chris was sweet, well-mannered, and undeniably polite.

Chris was also totally gay.

My rank as the youngest in our family might have left me ignored for years, but it did help me develop a valuable skill—acute observation. Secrets were always hiding in the small details. You merely had to look for them.

I wondered if that's why Chris hated me at first. I noticed things others missed, and he was worried about being found out. Eventually, he realized that I'd never disclose his secret even if I did figure it out.

I realized it fairly quickly after our courtship began. The way he tried *not* to stare at an attractive male and his fluidity with touching me. If you had sexual chemistry, there were nerves and anticipation when you got cozy with the person. It was easier to be affectionate when there was no attraction.

I watched him closely to understand. After all, New York City was open-minded and accepting. His parents might initially be reluctant, but they were loving people and would eventually accept him.

It seemed to be an intrinsic issue, not extrinsic.

Chris wasn't ready to come out, nor was he prepared for his life to drastically change. He was a jock and an involved member of the church. He had carved out an identity for himself, one he wasn't set to bid goodbye to.

Despite being from a humbler background, it didn't diffuse Chris' popularity with girls. He struggled to fend them off but could only do it for so long before rousing suspicion. Chris wasn't threatened by me as he subconsciously associated my nerdiness with being a non-sexual person.

Meanwhile, I was heartbroken after going through my fiasco with Brandon. I redirected my love toward someone who needed it to get through a difficult hump. Although platonic, love was love. We kissed—no tongue—to say hello and goodbye. And I was his friend who didn't mind being his beard, fending girls off while Chris came to terms.

Other than Gabby, Chris had become my closest friend and helped me move on. Plus, his presence appeased Raven's paranoia.

Raven's attitude changed considerably after meeting Chris. She used to text me every fifteen minutes if she knew boys were within my one-mile radius. If I was with Chris, she texted me in hourly increments.

He was a big guy and could easily ward off horny boys. But most importantly, I had zero sexual chemistry with him.

Chris was Raven's dream boyfriend for me.

I unlocked my phone and tapped on his name. He picked up on the first ring. "I was just thinking about calling you. Happy Friday."

I smiled. "Hello to you too."

"What are you doing this weekend?"

"Calc homework."

"Exciting," he said dryly.

"Isn't it? I'm also working on my Econ paper. And if I'm feeling really frisky, I might even prep for my AP Bio test."

Chris laughed. "How about I turn your exciting weekend into a boring one?"

"Hmm... I don't know." I picked up my pace as the cold air beat against my face. "What's more exciting than Calculus?"

"You're right. I can't compete with math homework, but if you want to take a break, come over this weekend. My parents invited you to dinner."

I would have screeched to a halt from the unprecedented suggestion had the wind not been knocked out of me. I collided against a hard mass and staggered backward. Two hands grabbed my waist, saving me from the concrete. I couldn't see the culprit as my scarf blew in every which way, blocking my vision.

The stranger steadied me by running two hands down my sides with firm strokes. It was an awfully intimate touch. Their presumptuous nature caught me off guard until I recognized the familiar rainforest smell.

"Fuck," I muttered, mouth slightly parted.

"Mia," Brandon addressed gruffly.

As soon as I heard his deep voice, I imagined covering my ears and screaming at the top of my lungs to drown out the sound. Every instinct screamed for me to make a run for it, to get away from him before he could inflict more damage.

I was on the path to reformation. Life had given me an olive branch to turn things around, and Brandon was here, like clockwork, to fuck it all up.

No more.

This obsession with Brandon Cooper was my downfall, and he had tormented me for the last time. I stared at him like he was the evil spirit I needed to ward off, wishing this was a figment of my imagination even though his hands on my waist dictated otherwise.

"Hello?" Chris' voice reminded me that I was still on an active call. The phone dangled loosely in my hand. "Mia, are you still there?"

I shook my head to expel the unwelcome thoughts. "Y-yeah," I managed to croak into the receiver. "Sorry, um..." My mind went blank as I tried to process Brandon's presence.

Unlike last time, he was clean shaved, and the unruly dark hair was tidier. His attire—black t-shirt, blue jeans, bomber jacket—was one I remembered from my childhood.

This was Brandon's go-to sex appeal look.

If I weren't convinced that he hated me, I would have wondered if Brandon had groomed himself before this run-in.

"Is everything okay?" Chris sounded concerned upon hearing my tone because that's the kind of man he was—a genuine one. Unlike the other one looming over me dangerously.

Brandon's eyes flickered to the phone as if just realizing that I was on a call. The volume was loud enough to hear muffled voices on the other end. Pushing against his chest, I sidestepped him, so he wouldn't hear Chris.

Brandon tilted his massive frame to block my sweet escape. "Not so fast."

"Who's that?" Chris asked.

Simultaneously, Brandon frowned. "Who are you speaking with?"

Instead of replying to Brandon, I spoke on the phone. "Do you mind if I call you—hey, what the hell?"

Brandon snatched the phone out of my hand and scowled at the screen. The way his face twitched upon reading the caller's identity had me diving for the device. He could see Chris' first AND last name. It was information I didn't want him to have.

"Mia?" Chris' voice came from a distance.

"Give it back," I hissed.

Brandon held the phone out of my reach. I might as well be fun-sized in comparison. A physical fight with him was futile. It was best to hang up before Brandon did any detrimental damage.

"Chris, I have to go. I'll call you back," I shouted, standing on my tippy toes.

"Okay," I faintly heard Chris' tentative response.

As Chris hung up, I called for as much composure as I could muster. Name-calling and anger served no purpose against a man like Brandon.

I glanced behind him. My house was a block away, so running into him couldn't be a coincidence. Was he waiting for me?

No way. Last I checked, Brandon and I were mortal enemies.

So, then what the fuck was he doing here?

I had every right to demand answers to such a simple question. I just needed to push the words out of my lips. *Why are you here?* "Is it embarrassing for you to be this obsessed with me?"

I assumed Brandon would snap at me. Instead, he smirked, his dark mood dissipating.

A set of devil eyes perused me slowly like they were busy taking their fill and would inform me when they were good and ready to move on. They were burning with either hunger or fury, or perhaps both.

I was in my school uniform—a white shirt, pleated skirt, boots, and a blazer. Nothing sexy to report, but his lewd ogling could have convinced me otherwise. He inspected every inch of my legs, neck, breasts. Repeatedly my breasts.

The initial nerves I had experienced returned tenfold. He was attempting to make me uncomfortable, and it was working. I pulled my blazer tighter against my chest and wiped my clammy hands on my skirt.

It was difficult not to crack under his scrutinizing intensity, and I used the term loosely.

This was ridiculous. He owed me an explanation about his presence. *Why are you here?* "If you stare any harder, you'll fall in love with me."

He kept staring, despite my factual words. Look it up. There was a direct correlation between eye contact and love.

"Look, I appreciate a good brooding and this whole *will they* or *won't they* thing we have going on, but perhaps you can schedule to stare into my eyes with heated passion for a later time. I'm busy at the moment." I held out my hand. "If you'll be so kind as to return my phone, I'll be on my way."

His eyes flickered to my outstretched palm, then back to my face. Unsurprisingly, he didn't comply.

"Phone, please."

"We need to talk." He dared to utter those words with a straight face.

No way.

Time and time again, I paid the price for any interaction with

Brandon. The first time I broke my cardinal rule and spoke to him, I lost my virginity, along with my sanity. The last time we spoke, Brandon burnt my book and the subsequent will to continue my visit with Milo. It had been weeks after the fact, and Milo was still shunning me.

I also lost my home in Paris, which wasn't Brandon's fault, but let's go ahead and blame it on him. I had no qualms scapegoating things on him. It was the universe's way of punishing me every time I betrayed Milo's trust for Brandon Stupid Cooper.

Brandon spoke as if I hadn't responded to his proposition. "I know a place nearby. We can talk there." He took five steps in the opposite direction. When I didn't move, he twisted his body. "You coming?"

"No, thank you," I replied tersely.

Brandon shrugged and continued. The way he arrogantly walked away, fully expecting me to change my mind, left me dumbfounded.

Did he really show up unannounced and then expect to have a civilized conversation? There was no way in hell I'd follow that stupid, conceited...

"Hey!" I called out, following after Brandon. I tugged at the sleeve of his jacket. It had no effect in stopping him, so I matched his brisk pace. "You have my phone."

"Yes." He patted his pocket.

Brandon rarely made a move without the guarantee of bending others to his will. He was walking away after gathering the necessary insurance.

Milo tracked my phone. Milo and Raven were synced to my Google Calendar that detailed my daily plans. I even listed church or plans to hang out with Chris so they could reach me.

If Brandon walked away with my phone, God knew where it'd end up. I was already on Milo's shit list. I had no interest in making it worse.

"Give me back my phone."

"I will... at the coffee shop," he replied easily.

"What coffee shop?"

Brandon nodded ahead. "I told you. The one nearby."

"I can't have coffee with you. I'm busy."

"You just got out of school."

"I have to study."

"But you already know everything."

"In that case, I don't *want* to have coffee with you."

"Too bad."

"Just give me back my damn phone," I snapped, scalp prickling with an oncoming migraine.

"I will. At the coffee shop," he reasserted.

I looked around the street, which was fairly empty, and I considered informing a neighbor about being mugged in broad daylight by my brother's best friend. Unfortunately, it'd only serve to embarrass me. I had promised to do better and be less reactive. I refused to lose my shit in the middle of the street because of Brandon.

We walked in silence. My blood was boiling from the sight of him, or perhaps I felt dizzy from shock. The last thing I expected was this encounter.

Brandon appeared unflustered by the piercing tension, which further pissed me off. He wordlessly held the door open as we reached the popular neighborhood café and followed me inside.

The shop was a fusion of art and culture. There were eclectic pieces all over the walls, and the owners regularly encouraged patrons to share their talents in front of a live audience.

A set up in the corner with mic and speakers indicated that either it was open mic night, or a local musician might play a few songs. The café was generally busy, but not so much this afternoon.

My eyes swept the room involuntarily. I prayed we didn't come across anyone who knew us. While coffee was an innocent enough outing, Milo would go ballistic if he found out about the companion. He might be giving me the cold shoulder at the moment, but it didn't change the situation.

A busboy I had seen before greeted me with a courteous smile when I passed, making me turn in his direction to return the favor. When I circled back to Brandon, I found him studying the busboy closely. Brandon's glare suddenly moved in my direction. Before I could utter a word, he roughly grabbed my hand, charging toward an unspoken destination.

Though I had maintained physical distance to minimize the outward appearance, Brandon was unperturbed by the risks involved. There was a pregnant pause when he herded me through a group of girls. They were assembled near the middle of the shop and did a double-take. It was difficult not to gape at the force of nature powering through their midst.

When we were younger, we teased Milo and Reid relentlessly for the groupies who chased after them. But Brandon was a category of his own.

Intimidating, he displayed every meticulous detail of a bad boy. The messy hair, the detached attitude, the ink—it was the holy trinity of danger and sex bottled inside one explosive package. He could hardly go somewhere without being ogled or eye-fucked.

However, they weren't only staring at Brandon.

The school uniform declared my youth, the lack of makeup and hair pulled into a braid only made me look younger. Whereas Brandon's natural confidence drew attention to the fact that he was a powerful, grown man.

Probing eyes tried to make sense of our odd pairing with stark differences in age and appearance since Brandon's possessive hold ruled out the possibility of us being related.

Luckily, the girls were discreet about their curiosity and politely looked away. Only one offender forgot to avert her eyes long after the socially acceptable grace period was over. She seemed awestruck, staring after Brandon like it was love at first sight.

I snorted inwardly.

A few months ago, I would have relished the idea of gouging this girl's eyes out. Now, all I could think was—*Good fucking luck.*

Unaware of the trail of broken hearts he was leaving behind, Brandon swiftly bypassed the restrooms before rounding the corner.

Suddenly, I knew exactly where he was headed.

A set of doors through this hallway opened to a separate room with a long table in the middle and scattered lounge chairs. No other decorative art pieces on the wall.

I often stationed a post in this room to study because I could hear the action from here, so I didn't feel alone. However, it wasn't loud enough to break my concentration.

The only souls I had seen here were the employees. Before today, I assumed no one else even knew about the café's hidden gem. And that's when I realized everything leading up to this moment was part of a plan designed by Brandon.

It was vindictive, calculative, and totally him.

Mia

DESPITE THEIR LOVE-HATE relationship and outlook in life, Milo and Brandon had more in common than the two realized. Not because they both attended Columbia or had extraordinary minds for business. It was the choreographed way they conducted themselves. Unlike me, neither of them was innately impulsive. They rationed their cards, bated their time, and attacked at the opportune moment.

Once, Milo and Brandon courted a potential investor. They were insistent about this particular investor being a great asset. Instead of taking any impromptu actions that might ruin their future chances, they did diligent research and found an Achilles heel. By the time they pitched a proposal, they had created an airtight plan and backed him into a corner, leaving the man with no option but to hop on board.

Similarly, Brandon had fashioned a custom trap leading up to this moment. He had predicted my every reaction, including an attachment to my phone. He knew I'd be uncomfortable being seen with him in public and chose a place with a hidden room—information he could've only been privy to by digging around.

The question remained. *Why is he doing this?*

Did he not have the chance to spew out enough venom before I kicked him out and needed to have the last word?

My heart didn't care for another bout of cruelty, but as long as he didn't burn more of my books, he could berate me and then be on his merry way.

I draped my backpack and scarf on the back of a chair and plopped down. "Talk."

Brandon settled across from me and picked up a menu from the table. "What's good here?"

"Nothing. Absolutely everything's disgusting here."

"They have iced coffee." He tapped the menu, unperturbed by my response.

"It's freezing outside." I paused. Who the hell cared about his temperature choice in drinks? "I don't want iced coffee. You wanted to talk, so talk."

"You're right. Let's do hot drinks."

"Brandon, what am I doing here?"

A waitress in her mid-thirties poked her head through the door frame. "Oh, I didn't know anyone was in here." She glided toward us with pen and notebook in hand. This place was just fancy enough to have servers who took orders at the table. "Has anyone helped you yet?"

"Not yet." Brandon dazzled her with a rare smile. He went as far as to engage in small talk. And he commented on the weather.

The fucking weather?!

Brandon could be charming when it suited him and purposefully chose to be an asshole at all other times. She was eating out of his palm and introduced herself, pointing out their most popular drink items.

"So, what can I get for you today?" she asked me, pen hovering over her notebook.

"A cell phone," I muttered.

Brandon's lips curved though he didn't take his eyes off the menu.

"Excuse me?" The waitress looked between us, wondering what the hell she walked into.

"Sorry. Nothing for me, but thank you."

"I'll take a regular coffee." Brandon inspected the menu closely before adding, "And she'll have the pumpkin spice latte with almond milk."

Another piece of information Brandon likely gathered during his investigation—my lactose intolerance and love for fall flavors.

I didn't understand this man's mind games or his angle.

Brandon ignored my bewilderment while inquiring about food recommendations. When the waitress mentioned they made scones from scratch—as long as we didn't mind the wait—he added two.

When she left, I became determined to resume our original conversation. "You wanted to talk." My foot tapped nervously under the table.

He leaned forward, pinning me in place with his eyes, well aware of the mesmerizing effect they had on others. He was too close for comfort. Snippets of our past dirty deeds flashed through my mind, and my thighs clenched at a particularly vulgar thought.

Unflinching, I stiffened the image. But Brandon's smirk told me he knew of my thoughts as I had held my breath for far too long.

"In Italy, you expressed an interest in creating your own beauty products. But Milo mentioned you planned to attend Yale in the fall, followed by a Doctorate in Psychology. You lied about your aspirations."

My jaw dropped. "*This* is what you want to discuss? I assumed you'd at least disclose your diabolical plan first."

The sides of his lips quirked. "My diabolical what?"

"You're an old family friend and could have easily dropped by my house under the pretense of being in the neighborhood. But no. You chose to stand in the cold, half a block away from my house, to *bump* into me," I made air quotes around the word bump. "Clearly, you didn't want to risk Milo finding out about this... rendezvous."

Brandon didn't deny or admit to the accusation, nor did he seem combative. It only alluded to my theory that Brandon was aware someone in the house reported back to Milo.

"And the reason you took my phone was because you knew Milo tracked it. Naturally, I'd do follow you for its safe return. Must I continue?"

Brandon appeared marginally fascinated. "Answer my question first, then we can discuss my..." he waved his fingers in the air to find the words.

"Diabolical plans," I said for his benefit. "What's the question?"

Brandon empaled me with his arresting crystal-blue orbs. "Did you lie to me about your ambitions?"

I looked straight ahead. "No. But my aspirations aren't practical to pursue. If I get my doctorate, I'll have a guaranteed six-figure salary right out of school."

"Sounds like something Milo would say."

I paused at Brandon's assessment. He was spot on. That statement was Milo's verbatim opinion. I often recycled it for my own purposes.

According to Milo and my other siblings, the dream life included a posh condo, an abundance of designer labels, and being part of New York's elites.

It vastly contrasted with my take. I preferred creative avenues, cozy homes and would have dyed my hair blue years ago if I didn't think it'd give my straight-edge brother a heart attack.

"Why aren't you pursuing makeup?" he asked again.

"I'm just finishing high school. Joining the workforce so early in life hardly makes sense."

"Then why not go to beauty school to learn the trade?"

"Having a traditional degree to fall back on makes more sense," I offered faintly.

"So, you *want* to go to college?"

"College is the bare minimum expected."

"That's not what I asked."

I grimaced at Brandon's not-so-subtle comment. My heart wasn't in it to contradict him convincingly.

When Milo insisted that Yale followed by a doctorate program was the natural course of action after graduation, I mindlessly aimed to achieve the goal. By the time I accumulated my own interests, Milo had already mapped out the next ten years of my life.

If I told him now that I'd rather pursue makeup than attend Yale, he'd look at me like I was mad. And Raven would list out logical reasons to demonstrate point by point why it was a crazy idea.

Too bad they didn't see eye to eye because they'd make an unstoppable good cop-bad cop duo. Together, they made for the perfect gilded cage.

Even as the thought crossed my mind, guilt overlapped it. Raven and Milo would take a bullet for me. They might be heavy-handed, but it came from a good place. And who knew? Perhaps once I started college, these silly notions would disappear.

Luckily, the waitress reappeared with a tray. I was grateful for the interruption and slumped into my chair while she distributed our drinks.

Brandon's steadfast eyes remained laser-focused on me. Ignoring the intensity, I concentrated on the foam leaf on my coffee. The pumpkin aroma was hard to resist, but it'd be a shame to spoil the Barista's latte art. I took a sip, careful not to ruin the shape, and was mildly pleased with my sipping skills when the leaf remained intact.

The waitress placed a cup of coffee in front of Brandon and the hot scones in the middle. Clearly, she had done her magic so the scones would come out at the same time.

She hovered expectantly, hoping for an acknowledgment of her excellent customer service. But Brandon didn't say thank you or smile. Instead, his eyes roamed my face in search of something else entirely.

"Thank you," I offered, even though she was only interested in Brandon's gratitude. I didn't miss the disappointment in her eyes upon realizing that the glimpse of charm Brandon had displayed was a complete farce. Her face fell, and she scooted away.

I gripped my cup with two hands, the silence stretching between us. For weeks, I was petrified of running into Brandon again. I had fortified my walls in the same way Brandon's tough exterior protected him. In the end, the experience wasn't excruciating, merely awkward.

Brandon reached for his coffee and sipped on it while I quietly picked at my scone.

"Are you going to answer my question?" he finally prodded, shoulders tensing under his jacket.

I smiled sadly, hoping to dismiss this topic. "Why are you suddenly so curious about my future?"

"Because I needed to understand how much of what you shared that weekend was true."

I frowned. "I have already answered your question. Your turn."

"My turn?"

I waved my hand like it was obvious. "Diabolical plan."

He opened his mouth but tensed when my phone buzzed, alerting me that a text had come through. My phone was in Brandon's pocket. I thought he might still hold it hostage, but he fished it out and handed it over.

Bitch Nanny #4: On my way.

I refused to dignify the spies Milo sent as anything more than Bitch Nannies 1 through 5 on my phone. It was beyond frustrating to spend the majority of my time alone yet have invisible strings control my every move.

By far, Claire (Nanny #4) was my least favorite. On the nights she came over to "check on Mom," she'd snoop through my room and confiscate my weed even though I had a prescription for it.

More than once, I had to sneak into the near-abandoned house on our block and hide my weed. If I wasn't at home, as listed on my calendar, she'd call Milo to rat me out.

I sprang to my feet. "I have to go."

It was moments before Brandon reacted to my announcement. He appeared to be biting his tongue, and I half expected him to argue. Instead, he pushed his chair back. Reaching into his wallet, Brandon threw two twenty-dollar bills on the table.

I gathered my things from the back of the chair, though faintly aware that he was rounding the table, his frame steadily gaining distance.

He had gone to extensive lengths to secure a private conversation, the type of investment he generally reserved for his most VIP clients. Obviously, he had brought me here for a purpose. A man of Brandon's stature wouldn't have taken such measures otherwise. I had a gut feeling that I wouldn't be leaving this place without hearing it.

Only when I realized he was much too close for comfort did the clutter-free room suddenly appear claustrophobic. Ignoring his looming presence, I fiddled with the lining of my bag instead.

He nodded at the phone in my hand. "That boy you were speaking to, Chris Allen. Who is he?" he asked with a straightforwardness that turned my blood cold.

I instantly sought to retort that it was none of his business. However, since it was my first impulse, it likely wasn't a tactful approach.

My eyes raked over Brandon's face to understand the purpose behind his inquiry. "A boy from church." The whole truth was awfully detail-oriented. And I couldn't disclose Chris' truth, especially since he had never explicitly disclosed it himself.

"A boy who's interested in you?" he alleged in a deceptively even tone.

I closed my eyes and prayed for patience against Brandon's massive ego. He expected me to become an old cat lady because he found me repulsive? Whatever game he was cooking up, I had no interest in playing.

My eyes flew open when he yanked at my braid. A silent reminder that he wasn't going anywhere without an answer.

"If Chris were to have any interest in me, he's entitled to those feelings."

For a moment, Brandon said nothing else. I would have considered his reaction anti-climactic were it not for the fact that anger was straining through every one of his taut muscles. And he was a little too quiet.

Some said no news was good news. I disagreed. The quietest men in my world were the most ruthless ones. Lack of a knee-jerk reaction was always foreboding to something worse. I could no longer hear anyone else in the café either. All the patrons must have predicted the same ominous threat and cleverly scattered.

"For his own good, I hope that isn't true." His strangely soft voice did nothing to fool me. Brandon's callous threat was very clear. Snippets of dark emotions leaked out of his stoic, blank eyes.

"Chris is just a friend," I said hurriedly.

Brandon scoffed like he didn't believe me, and that's when I realized he already knew the truth. "Then you're going to tell him it's a friendship you are no longer able to maintain."

Fumes bubbled from my insides. It wasn't enough to berate me and burn my book to scraps. Now he was showing up unannounced and acting like my keeper. Even the newly diplomatic Mia had her limits.

"Go to hell. You don't get to dictate my life after realizing there're other men out there. And believe it or not, I don't even have to trick any of them into sleeping with me."

It happened so fast that I didn't have the chance to react. He grabbed my braid to wrench up my head, lips hovering inches away. My heart slammed against my ribcage, the blood in my veins fizzling.

"If you slept with him... scratch that... if he so much as touched you, I'll make you pay." There was a dark cloud hovering over Brandon, but it was the storm in his eyes that gave him away. They flared lethally, his intimidating size crowding me as he whispered, "But it'll pale in comparison to what I'll do to him."

His threats had goaded me into the exact admission he had hoped for.

A chill trickled down my spine. Brandon wasn't the type of boy who shared his toys even after he was done with them.

Brandon slowly gathered himself. With his eyes still locked on my face, he unclenched the grip on my hair and dragged his fingers down the column of my neck so languidly that it sent a shudder through me. I took a deep breath to steady myself and inadvertently inhaled whiffs of his clean scent.

After an eternity, he dropped his hand, prompting me to do the same with my gaze.

"You're going to tell that boy you can't see him anymore," he said calmly.

Like hell. Chris was my only friend.

Brandon picked up on the defiance in my aggressive stance. "You'll regret it if I find out otherwise."

My eyes widened, but I didn't argue. I'd let him believe anything so that I could leave. I slung my bag over my shoulder.

"One last thing," he spoke before I could bolt.

I waited, hand twisting around the straps of my backpack.

"We had some issues come up with our office space and have to temporarily shut it down. All the coders and staff will be working from home."

I frowned.

So? Lots of tech companies worked remotely, and some didn't

even have a central location. What the hell did that have to do with anything?

"It's inconvenient because the next few weeks are crucial. We have a massive deadline coming up to open our California branch. All the business partners have to work around the clock. Night and day."

I had heard about their plans to expand to the West Coast. It's supposed to be their most time-consuming project to date.

"We can only keep up a schedule like that if we work and sleep out of the same location. Even a cab ride back and forth is invaluable time we could be using."

Oook.

"Problem is, there is only one person with a home office and a house large enough to accommodate the four of us."

Dread built inside me as I realized what was coming next.

"Looks like I'll be moving in with you, little Bunny. Milo's coming home too."

Oh, God.

I could hardly stand the guilt around Milo for a few minutes, let alone weeks with Brandon under the same roof.

Not to mention, Brandon didn't pay attention to his surrounding, tuning everyone else out because he cared for no one. However, he ALWAYS paid attention when it mattered to him.

This time, he'd be paying attention to me to solidify his theory that I orchestrated it all.

Brandon was smart. Really fucking smart. Other than Milo, he was the only one that ever challenged me. If we lived together, and he was actively paying attention, he'd figure out that I knew way too much about him than I should.

What if he got suspicious and hired a private investigator to look into my past? He'd find out about my stalking within a jiffy.

There was a paper trail of all the times I flew to Nice and stayed in the same hotel as he did.

Not to mention, my credit card transactions from the restaurants he frequented. I'd sit in the booth behind him while he ate a meal. How long before he looked into his own transaction history and matched the dates?

And let's not forget Uber receipts during the times I followed him from Point A to Point B.

Oh, God. Stalking was totally illegal. Would he indict me for it?

"Why are you doing all of this?" I whispered, horrified.

"Because you set me up."

"Don't say that."

"How can I not when your actions can cost me everything I've built over the years?"

"But no one even knows about what happened between us."

"You know about it. If the word ever got out, no one would care that I didn't know you were only sixteen."

"I won't tell anyone."

He shrugged. "Guess I'm not feeling so trusting and would rather keep a closer eye on you."

"Why do you think I'll screw you over after all this time?" I asked, frustrated.

He took a step forward, grazing the back of his knuckles against my cheek, and leaned it to whisper, "Because you already have."

WANT MORE?

Continue reading Mia and Brandon's in Discord: https://amzn.to/3rgdlbj

Turn the page for a sneak peek of Discord, Book 2 of the Chaos Series.

Discord: Sneak Peek

Brandon

"I'm busy. Make it quick." Milo's No.1 response made it painfully easy to crack his veneer, egging me on.

"What's the forecast for today in Chicago?"

"I'm going to hang up if you don't get to the point."

"Would you describe it as sweater weather?"

Milo was quiet on the other side. He didn't hang up, but I could taste his frustration through the phone.

I had been pushing his buttons more frequently as of late. Misery liked company, and since it felt like Milo had robbed me of everything, he owed it to me to join this miserable club. I was tired of suffering alone.

I wasn't sure which emotion would take the lead if I ever saw ~~Maya~~ Mia again—bewilderment, anger, or lust. Turned out that all three intermingled to create an explosive mix ready to obliterate everything in the vicinity. To have found her again, my last remaining semblance, only to give it up because of fucking Milo. For I might have complicated feelings about our friendship, but even I couldn't justify chasing after his teenage sister as obscure.

It was wrong. Plain and simple.

"I'm assuming Aldo didn't give you the news you had hoped for about that girl."

I gritted my teeth.

Perhaps I *could* justify it. It'd be so easy to turn the fucker's world upside down. Sometimes my hands visibly shook for control to abstain from doing so. Especially on the days he played dirty to get a rise out of me.

"I'll take your silence as my answer." He sounded bored. "But I fail to understand how moving to California will make things better or why you are doing this in the first place."

Because that's how much space was required to fight the urge to seek *her* out. "Because then I don't have to live in the same city as you," I said with equal amounts of ennui. "Just the thought makes me happy."

"If it makes you so happy, why did you take it out on our routers?"

Instead of responding, I ran my fingers through my hair.

After our altercation in Nice, I returned to my monotone life with lethal fury inside my chest. I had fought hard to escape my past and hadn't made a single mistake in ten years.

Then Hurricane Mia hit me—category infinity. The little attention seeker catfished me. Served me right. Women were filled with deceit, and I should have known better than to let one of them under my skin.

For too long, I had put my life on hold because of her, convinced I hadn't conjured up a weekend. Turned out it was imaginary. I had spent months obsessed with a fictional character. I had exercised considerable lapses in judgment for a girl so insignificant it was damn near infuriating. Not to mention unattainable.

It wasn't just about waiting for Mia until she turned eighteen. Milo had witnessed too many of my errors to rectify. After Mom passed away, I indulged in lines of blow, alcohol, reckless behavior, impulsive trips, irresponsible tattoos, and even jail time in Nice. All around bad choices and the worst choice for his baby sister.

My only redeeming quality was my aversion to being a man whore. But it wasn't enough of a saving grace, not for Mia—Milo's pride and joy.

If I pursued her, I'd have to go to war with her brother no matter what age she happened to be. Ultimately, it'd be all for nothing because she'd still pick *him* over me. She confirmed it herself.

The latter left me resentful of Milo. It also made me decide to move to California.

Bitter irony filled me.

How long had I searched for her? What had I not done to find her? Tracked anyone in Paris matching her description or using that alias. Recounted my every move for clues. All dead ends, only to find out she had been under my nose this entire time.

Utterly absurd because finding her had forced me to put the distance of a country between us. That's why I spearheaded this project to open a new branch on the West Coast. Otherwise, my resolve would break before she turned eighteen. If I waited to pursue her, I'd be able to face myself in the mirror, though Mia's allegiance remained the bigger hindrance.

Despite the rational decision, pestering thoughts of her refused to leave my mind. One fucking weekend had fueled an obsession. I had dreamt of it and replayed the moments repeatedly to relive them inside my mind. I had never wanted something so bad. It left a physical gnawing under my skin, rendering me incapable of an ounce of peace until finding myself at the Sinclair home.

"Brandon?" Reid held open the door, surprised. Rightfully so. "Hey, long time. Come on in."

"Hey, man." With trepidation, I followed him inside. My eyes inadvertently swept the place, searching for a glance of golden hair.

"Since when do you migrate out of Noho?"

I put on a smile. Reid was tolerable enough. It was a shame he had a pathological liar for a sister. "Whenever your brother is in town."

"Milo isn't in town." Reid tilted his head, hinting I should be privy to this knowledge.

I was. "Are you kidding me?" I glanced around, irritated. "My P.A. must have read his schedule wrong. I'm going to fire her ass."

Reid shrugged easily. "No harm. You are already here. Stay for a drink."

I glanced at my watch contemplatively, careful not to appear overly enthusiastic. "Guess I can stay for one drink. Whiskey if you have it."

Reid walked to the globe bar to find a bottle and tipped it for a generous pour. "You know, there is a little thing called a calendar to schedule your appointments. Maybe look into this concept instead of firing your PA."

The ice clinked as we brought our drinks together in cheers. "I don't condone such witchcraft," I replied dryly.

Reid laughed. "Then you should talk to my sister." My ears perked, and I stopped breathing altogether. "Raven put Mia's entire life on a calendar, then synced it to her phone in case Mia forgot a tutoring session or extracurricular."

I stood by my assessment from once upon a time—that poor kid. All the same, I wished he'd show me said calendar for Mia's current whereabouts. Impatience thrummed through me, and I couldn't keep my mouth from twisting. "Interesting."

Reid shook his head with a sardonic smile. "It's a bit intense if you ask me. Raven even lists Mia's dates with her boyfriend on that calendar."

My blood ran cold. The smile vanished off my face, whiskey glass swirling in my hand. It took significant effort to feign enough indifference to speak. "Boyfriend? Isn't Mia a little too young for that?"

"As her brother, I agree. But I once told Milo to fuck off when he banned my teenage hormones from copulating. It'll be worse if we don't get on board."

Forging a smile, I sipped on my drink, saying nothing more. Fire was burning through my blood by the time I returned to the office. Tiny red dots distorted my vision at the idea of another man's hands on her. And when one of the techs asked me to look into at a router issue, I took a bat to every piece of equipment stored in our office basement.

She ruined my plans. Fucking Mia Sinclair.

No idea why the hell I had gone to her house in the first place.

Probably eager to merely surround myself with a warmth that had been ripped away. Instead, I was served a fresh dose of reality.

A few measly weeks after our encounter in Nice shouldn't have been enough time for Mia to find a boyfriend. The news came as a punch to the gut. Actually, it was a shot to the chest. I had been so forlorn in my anger that I didn't realize Mia hadn't given me a second thought. She got away with living out her weird book-based fantasy while forcing me into these goddamn feelings I couldn't shake.

I ground my teeth to keep the lethal darkness from consuming me, but it didn't help. With a disgruntled breath, I took it out on her brother instead. "Are you still harping over your precious routers? I'm paying to have them replaced. How about I also write you a check to never bring it up again?"

"That's the problem with people like you. Entitlement. Money doesn't buy every—"

Dear fucking God. "If you're done," I cut him off sharply, "can we strategize for the California project?"

Milo sighed. "I assume you are calling me because you have suggestions."

"Yes."

He waited patiently on the other side of the phone.

"Instead of having two separate West and East Coast locations, I think we should downsize our New York office to only house our equipment."

"Very different from your original proposal. What changed?"

Your sister got a boyfriend.

I also broke all our routers. Milo hadn't been back and wasn't aware of the extent of the damages. Our current bandwidth could no longer support our sizeable staff. Most of them were already working from home.

"West Coast is better for the tech industry. Makes more sense to move our base there rather than paying for two hefty leases. Not to mention, working from home hasn't affected our team's performance." All of it was true.

"Do you think Jaci and Alexa will agree?"

"Yes." Because I already passed it by them.

"Okay. Let's figure out the logistics then."

"Without an office space, we need to decide where to work out of? We have a rigorous schedule over the next few months."

Personal reasons aside, expanding to the West Coast was once in a lifetime opportunity. The prospect required our undivided attention with all hands-on deck.

"It'll be difficult to keep things seamless during this transition if the four of us aren't together around the clock. The best option is to share temporary living accommodations."

Another pregnant pause on the other side. Milo was considering my suggestion. However, I needed him to take the last leap.

"I think my place makes the most sense—"

"My parents' brownstone," Milo declared like the little authoritarian I expected him to be.

I smiled.

The bizarre idea had been brewing since I met with Mia at that café. Part of it was to keep her from seeing someone else, but there was another reason. Mia didn't seem happy with her current life. Much like myself.

I pressed Mia about how much of what she had shared in the cottage was true. She claimed not to have lied. Much to my chagrin over Mia concealing her identity, I believed the rest to be true. She wasn't happy with the current path forced upon her but didn't know how to change her destiny.

Clearly, I lacked rationality around that girl's potent scent. Without confirming it with Milo, I declared my intent to move into the Sinclair home.

Luckily, Milo was predictable, though I put up a deliberate protest. "I prefer to work out of my home."

"That's not happening. You live in a condo. We need more space. There's already a home office set up at my parents' brownstone, along with a separate apartment for you, Jaci, and Alexa. So let me know when you want to move in."

I sighed reluctantly. "Couple of weeks."

A couple of weeks to talk myself out of this insane plan. I wanted to move across the country to be away from her. Now I was manipulating everyone to live two floors down from Mia.

The Sinclair home was comprised of two giant brownstones connected to make for one lavish mansion. The split-level was a floor below the family brownstone and had its own entrance. Milo's family lived beyond their means, and Milo... well, he was a sucker, working like a dog instead of denying them. That family was filled with drama, and the living situation was far from ideal. However, I couldn't take two more seconds of picturing another man's grubby hands on Mia without doing something lethal.

On some level, I also wanted to punish her for working me out of her system while I was drowning. She needed to join this miserable club so we could be unhappy together—a righteous payback for the fabrications.

After hanging up with Milo, an email came through from Aldo. It was the request I had put in for Chris Allen.

When I first met Mia, I was convinced she was my punishment from the powers above. Retribution for Dad. It ended up being true because Mia turned me into a person worse than my father. The thought alone should be enough to let her go and allow her to be with someone her own age. Such as Chris Allen.

My chest burned at the idea, and I forwarded the email to Mia.

Finish reading Mia and Brandon's story in Discord: amzn.to/3PDUUHm

----

A review for an author is like leaving a tip for your server. If you enjoyed Brandon & Mia's story, consider leaving me a review on the following sites:

Goodreads: bit.ly/3yI9k1m

Amazon: bit.ly/OC1zon

Afterword

Thank you for giving me a chance by reading this book. Sign up for my Newsletter for a deleted scene. Find me on Facebook for signed paperbacks, giveaways, and more.

A review for an author is like leaving a tip for your server. If you enjoyed Brandon & Mia's story, please consider leaving me a review on Goodreads or Amazon.

Don't forget to read Discord, the second and final part of this duet.

About the Author

Drethi Anis is a dark, contemporary author and prefers to write anti-heroes. Drethi's stories will always have angst, obsession, and a dark twist. Though toxic love and darkness are major players in her books, romance is still a priority. Stay tuned for future releases by signing up for her Newsletter. Connect with the author directly:

Reader Group

Instagram

Linktree

Also by Drethi Anis

THE QUARANTINE SERIES

QUARANTINED

ISOLATION

ESSENTIAL

THE QUARANTINE BOX SET 1-3 & BONUS SCENES

THE CHAOS SERIES

ORGANIZED CHAOS

DISCORD

THE SEVEN SINS SERIES

LUST

Printed in the USA
CPSIA information can be obtained
at www.ICGtesting.com
LVHW011934010124
767909LV00048B/1149